GOOD PUCK CHARM

(A Silverpeak Sabres College Hockey Romance — Book One)

AUDREY SHINE

Audrey Shine

Audrey Shine is author of the JULIET PAGE COZY MYSTERY series, comprising five books (and counting); and of the new SILVERPEAK SABRES ROMANCE series, comprising five books (and counting).

Audrey would love to hear from you, so please visit www.audreyshineauthor.com to receive free ebooks, hear the latest news, and stay in touch.

ISBN: 978-1-0943-8546-4

BOOKS BY AUDREY SHINE

JULIET PAGE COZY MYSTERY
A HARDCOVER HOMICIDE (Book #1)
A LETHAL LEXICON (Book #2)
A VOLUME IN VENGEANCE (Book #3)
A TYPESET TRAGEDY (Book #4)
A FATAL FOOTNOTE (Book #5)

SILVERPEAK SABRES ROMANCE
GOOD PUCK CHARM (Book #1)
PUCKER UP (Book #2)
NAUGHTY & ICE (Book #3)
PUCK OF THE DRAW (Book #4)
HEARTS ON ICE (Book #5)

CHAPTER ONE: LILY

The first time I walk into the office of the Silverpeak Sabres as an adult, it feels like stepping onto hallowed ground. I can almost hear the echo of hockey pucks smacking against the boards and the distant cheer of a crowd that lives for the game. My excitement is a live wire under my skin, prickling with every step I take deeper into the place where my love for hockey took root.

"Morning!" I greet the administrative assistant, my grin probably too wide to be considered professional. But enthusiasm isn't something I can—or care to—temper.

"Morning, Lily," she responds, her smile genuine but cut with the weariness that seems to hang over the whole office like a cloud. Even first thing in the morning, I've noticed the whole vibe is just a *little sad.*

It's a homecoming of sorts, returning to Silverpeak, the Michigan town where my father's skates once carved the ice before his dreams were dashed by a cruel twist of fate. Where my childhood was spent strapping on skates of my own, all the way up through high school. Now, in my twenties and grasping for any marketing position that would have post-graduation me when the ink is still wet on my degree, I shake off the nostalgia; I'm not here to relive history—I'm here to make it.

"Ah, Lily Morgan," Mr. Thompson's voice booms as he emerges from his office just as I come onto the main office floor. His presence is commanding even without the backdrop of trophies and framed jerseys that adorn his walls. "Welcome aboard."

"Thank you, Mr. Thompson," I say, extending a hand that he envelops with a firm, practiced grip.

"Please, call me Frank," he insists, waving me into his office that smells faintly of leather and old coffee. "I'm glad to have you. The school plans to keep expanding the athletic department, so we're trying to get ahead of that with personnel. I…was sorry to hear about your dad. Local hero."

I have to push down the know that forms in my throat, forcing a smile. It's been two years, but it never gets easier to be reminded that my hero hadn't beaten cancer. "Thank you. I'm sure he'd be so happy to have been remembered here."

Frank clears his throat and gestures to a chair, where I sit. He takes a stack of papers out of his desk and hands them across. "Here's the welcome packet. Tech will set up your workstation by tomorrow, but the passwords for WIFI, the sports archives, and the staff directory are there. Play roster, too. We've got our work cut out for us. The team's performance has been...less than stellar. We need a fresh perspective, someone who can light a fire under this community's spirit—and put their butts back in the stands."

"Consider it done," I reply, though I know it will be anything but easy. "I've got some ideas that I think could really—"

"Good, good," Frank nods eagerly, then glances at his watch. "But first, we have a pregame team meeting in ten minutes. You should sit in, get a feel for the dynamics on and off the ice."

"Wouldn't miss it," I say, already plotting.

He smiles. "Be right back."

Frank leaves me to my own devices, and I immediately take my laptop out of my bag, diving into the archives. I flick through digital files, absorbing the history of triumphs long celebrated and defeats not so easily forgotten. Then, recent social media and news coverage. The fan base for the school is passionate yet dwindling, despite Silverpeak reaching that coveted D1 status—and figuring out why is a challenge I'm more than ready to take head-on.

My laptop screen is a collage of statistics and social media feeds when Frank reappears. "Lily, ready to meet the team?"

"Absolutely," I respond, snapping my laptop shut with a decisive click. I stand, straighten my jacket, and follow him down the hallway, my heart keeping time with the staccato of my heels on the linoleum floor. This is it—the first play of the game, and I'm determined to make it count.

***

I step into the locker room, which is dim and buzzing with voices, a mix of sweat and steam in the air. The walls show off banners from past wins, but the vibe here is more about recent losses than those big moments. I remind myself why I'm here: this team needs a new spark.

Silverpeak hasn't always been a D1 school, and there hasn't always been interest in the sports programs here. But since I left to go to school myself, the campus has explode din terms of student body numbers and the programs that are offered. And just a couple years back, the school hit all the D1 requirements—bam, instant rise in attention *and* pressure. We haven't always been the best, but with all these guys, we've got a real shot at turning things around. And I'm here to lead the way.

"Everyone, meet Lily Morgan," Mr. Thompson calls out, "our new marketing expert."

I get a mix of nods and shrugs. The room's full of different guys, all players I've familiarized myself with from the roster online, and I'm sure each has his own story. Ethan Scott, one of the defensemen, gives me a friendly smile, his blue eyes warm.

Next to him, Noah Jensen stands tall. He's another defenseman—looking disciplined, but you can tell he's got secrets just by looking into his eyes.

Lucas Ford, our star forward, is leaning against his locker, eyeing me, curious but a bit doubtful. His charm's obvious, even without a word.

Alex "Ace" Allister, the left winger, has kind eyes that are making me feel a bit more at ease.

Dylan "Daredevil" Donovan, with his dark looks, watches from the back, tattoos peeking out—clearly the guy who loves living on the edge.

Sean Murphy, our goalie, is like a tower, calm and strong, nodding at me like he's saying *we've got this* without speaking a word.

Damon Hayes and Jamie Carlson share a quick look, one full of hope and the other worry. Damon's the city boy turned athlete, sharp and ready to prove himself, while Jamie's the friendly face everyone likes, bringing that team spirit.

Sebastian Costa, standing a bit off to the side, watches me warily, clearly not sold on the whole marketing thing yet.

But it's Marco Silvestri, the hotshot forward, who really grabs my attention. Leaning against the lockers, arms crossed, he's impossible to ignore. Even before he speaks, you know he's someone who leads naturally.

The moment Marco Silvestri leans against those lockers, every bit of the dimly lit room seems to fade into the background, drawing all my attention to him. He stands there with an effortless ease that belies the strength underneath, a presence that's impossible to ignore. Marco, with his Italian heritage coloring every inch of him, from the olive skin that seems to glow even under the harsh fluorescent lights to the dark, tousled hair that looks like it's perpetually just been ruffled by a helmet or a hand running through it in frustration—or maybe just for the sheer pleasure of feeling its texture.

His eyes, though, they're something else entirely—deep brown, almost black, with a mischievous glint that suggests he's always one step ahead in any conversation, always ready with a comeback or a challenge. There's an intensity there too, a depth that makes you wonder what thoughts swirl behind those gaze. It's captivating, drawing you in, making you want to dive deep into those pools and discover all the secrets they guard.

And when he smiles, it's not just any smile. It's a smirk that makes promises, one corner of his mouth tugging up higher than the other, as if he's in on a joke that the rest of us haven't quite caught onto yet. It's the kind of smile that could easily infuriate if you're on the receiving end of a smart remark, but for now, it's utterly charming, disarming even.

There's an undeniable allure to Marco Silvestri—rugged athleticism and a sharp wit, all wrapped up in a package that's as compelling as it might be confounding. It's not just his looks; it's the air of confidence, the assurance of someone who knows exactly who he is and what he's capable of. And from where I'm standing, it's impossible not to be a little bit in awe, a little bit captivated, and maybe more than a little interested in everything he represents.

"Marketing, huh?" Marco's voice cuts through, clearly doubting. "How's that supposed to help us win?"

"By getting the stands full, boosting the team's morale, and making wins feel inevitable," I answer, holding his gaze. "Having the town behind you can make a huge difference."

He smirks a bit. "Sounds too good to be true."

"Well, believe it or not, you'll see it work," I tell him, keeping up the banter. "As long as you work." His doubt doesn't scare me off—it just makes me want to prove it all the more. I left this city to go to college, and, sure, my greatest brush with hockey fame was youth leagues, but Dad made sure I developed a love for the game. Besides, banter is a language I know well, a tool as sharp as any blade on the ice.

Marco's mouth snaps open, and I can tell that whatever he's going to say next isn't going to be too polite. Before things can escalate, Ethan Scott steps between us, his towering frame a meditator's barrier. "Let's give her a chance, Marco. Could be the game-changer we need."

Ethan Scott—defensemen, if I'm remembering everyone right—is tall and looks like he can handle anything that comes his way, including our little argument. His sandy-blond hair is a bit messy. When he looks at me, his bright blue eyes are full of understanding, without needing to say anything. Then he turns to Marco with a look that's serious but not angry, just enough to stop the argument in its tracks.

He gives us a quick smile that makes me feel a bit better instantly. It's a warm, genuine smile that seems to say everything's going to be okay. Ethan seems such a contrast to Marco—like he doesn't need to be loud or bossy; people just want to follow him because they trust him.

Marco shrugs noncommittally, but I can tell he's already reassessing, his mind never far from strategy—on or off the ice.

The tension in the room resolves, and Thompson claps his hands. "Okay, team. On the ice! Game time!"

***

The rink is colder than I remember, the chill biting through my jacket as I perch on the bleachers, watching the team glide across the ice. They move with power and grace, but the cohesion I'd expect from a team with their history isn't quite there. It's like watching a symphony where each musician plays a different tune.

"See something you can market?" Marco's voice comes from in front of me, teasing yet curious. I look up to see him at the rink's edge, grinning that barbed grin.

"Potential," I say simply, looking back at the other players. "And plenty of work to do."

"So you're an optimist, huh?"

"It's not optimism; it's faith in hard work," I reply, scribbling down notes on my tablet—*positioning, teamwork, cohesion.*

"Faith..." Marco echoes, the word hanging between us, heavy with unspoken disdain. It's clear he's a man who believes in earning his keep, in the tangible push of body against body, stick against puck. Not in feelings or faith.

"Exactly," I say, finally looking at him. "With a little faith and a lot of elbow grease, we'll turn this around."

His brown eyes meet mine, and for a fleeting moment, I see the barest hint of belief flicker within them before he pushes off of the wall and skates away.

The scoreboard mocks us with its glaring red digits. Zero to eight. It's not just a loss; it's a massacre. I lean forward in my seat, feeling the collective disappointment rolling off the stands—which are only half-full, if we're being generous—like a thick fog. The final buzzer sounds, and the ice seems to swallow the groans and curses of the crowd.

"Brutal, right?" A voice heavy with heartbreak speaks from next to me. I turn to find a middle-aged man wearing a jersey that has seen better days, his face painted in our team's colors. "Name's Jeff. Die-hard fan since '86. I seen you makin' notes during the game. New assistant coach?"

"Lily," I introduce myself, offering a smile that I feel doesn't quite reach my eyes. "New to the marketing team."

"Marketing, huh?" Jeff muses, scratching his stubble. "Well, you've got your work cut out for ya. This town lives and breathes hockey. But this..." He gestures at the clearing players, his hand slicing through the air with finality. "This isn't our hockey."

"I know," I agree. "We're going to change that."

"Good luck," he says with a weary chuckle. "You'll need it."

I stand up, my mind already racing with ideas as I descend the bleachers and use the staff hallway to get away from the rink. The energy of the loss, although somber, has sparked something within me—an urgency, a challenge I can't wait to tackle head-on.

Back at the office, my laptop screen glows from its place in the clutter of papers and scattered notes from earlier. I dive into our social media profiles, the engagement—or lack thereof—painting a pretty dire picture. The comments sections are battlefields where fans like Jeff, the die-hards—fight against naysayers who echo over and over the Sabres are sunk. And even those few posts are like echoes in an empty room.

We have to get people interested again, I think, tapping my pen against my lips.

Campaigns begin to form in my mind: player spotlights, behind-the-scenes footage, interactive Q&As.

"Local businesses," I mutter, jotting down names of places I remember from growing up here. I'll check to see if they're still around. My dad had a lot of friends in the business community, a lot of old favors that I might be able to call in. "Community leaders..." More jotting. The list is gaining potential. "We need everyone on board."

I sketch out ideas for open-house events, imagining the rink bustling with excited fans, autograph signings that bridge the gap between the players and the community, charity matches that show the heart beneath the jerseys. My brain rushes three steps ahead, planning meetings, envisioning partnerships that could give us the visibility we desperately needed. I'm so lost in brainstorming that I almost don't hear when my phone buzzes with an email from Mr. Thompson.

I'll be back in the office in ten. Quick chat?

I reply in the affirmative.

My fingers dance across the laptop keys, each click a building block in the blueprint for revival. The college hockey team's office is my workshop, and I, Lily Morgan, am crafting more than just a marketing plan—I am engineering hope.

I hear the main bullpen door open.

"Mr. Thompson," I call out through my open office door. He strolls into the room, his curiosity obviously piqued by the energy buzzing from my corner. His gaze sweeps over the mock-ups sprawled across the desk.

"Well, I was coming to see if our loss had already scared you off," he quips. "But show me what you've got, Morgan." He leans forward, hands clasped behind his back like a coach ready to evaluate his star player's game plan.

"Right." Clearing my throat, I stand, feeling the familiar rush I had once known on the ice—the thrill of a challenge. "The Sabre's image needs a facelift, sure, but what we really need is to create a deeper connection with our fan base. You're losing them, and it's creating a ripple effect. We're going to tell our story, the players' stories—humanize them."

I tap my laptop screen, where a collage of candid shots and action stills brings life to names and numbers. "We'll launch a series of featurettes, 'Beyond the Ice', diving into their lives, struggles, and triumphs. Fans love an underdog, and we've got a team full of them."

I think of Marco—and how he'll probably roll his eyes at this suggestion. I don't know why, but the thought of his opposition grates on me. And it hasn't even happened yet.

"Interesting," Mr. Thompson murmurs, his head tilting slightly as he considers my words.

"Next," I continue, flipping to a graph that showed engagement analytics, "we revamp our social media strategy. Live Q&As, game-day vlogs, interactive polls—we make the fans feel like they're part of the locker room huddle."

"And the community?" He leans in, eyes sharp. "We used to have twice the sponsors that we have now."

"Local partnerships are key," I say, pointing to a list of businesses and potential sponsors. "Imagine the team volunteering, attending town events, becoming local heroes off the ice as well as on it. It builds pride—and ticket sales. And with attention comes sponsorships. Businesses want to be associated with positive press that redirects to them."

"Ms. Morgan," Mr. Thompson breaks into a grin that stretches wide across his face, "you've done all this, and it's just lunchtime!"

His approval is a blast of cold air against my flushed cheeks, as invigorating as stepping onto the rink. "Well, you know what they say—the early bird gets the... puck?"

He chuckles, shaking his head at my attempt at humor. "Keep this up, and you might just turn this ship around. Go take a break—you've earned it."

"Thanks, Mr. Thompson. I will." I power down my laptop and collect my thoughts, along with my jacket. "Is Granny's still open?"

He nods. "Yep. Best burgers in the tri-state."

Perfect. The knowledge that Granny's Kitchen is still operating gives me hope for my list of potential partners for the Sabres.

As I reach the door, Thomspon calls out to me. I stop and look back.

"I think your pop would be real proud of you, Lily," he says.

My chest pinches. "Thanks."

Stepping out into the brisk midday air, which stings a little in my watery eyes, I make my way to the local diner that was a fixture of my childhood.

The bell above the door chimes softly as I push into Granny's Kitchen, the familiar sound transporting me back to a simpler time. I pause just inside the doorway, allowing my eyes to adjust to the cozy interior, bathed in the warm glow of overhead lights. It's been years since I last set foot in here, yet everything from the checkered curtains to the worn, cushioned booths feels exactly as I left it.

The scent of freshly brewed coffee and bacon sizzling on the griddle fills the air, mingling with the soft murmur of conversation from the scattered patrons. It's lunchtime, and the place is comfortably busy, alive with the sound of clinking silverware and the occasional laughter.

I take a deep breath, the nostalgic aroma evoking memories of weekend mornings spent with my dad, huddled over plates of pancakes drowning in syrup, and after-school burgers that tasted like perfection.

"Table for one, hon?" The voice, warm and slightly husky, belongs to Martha, the ever-present waitress who seems not to have aged a day. Her smile is as welcoming as I remember, her eyes crinkling at the corners in genuine delight. "Lily! Why, Lily Morgan. Didn't know you were back in town. Haven't seen you since you lit off for college."

"Just one," I confirm, returning her smile—and her sudden hug—as I waver between excitement and a tinge of sadness for the years that have slipped away. "And it's good to be back. How are you?"

She leads me to a booth by the window, the one that used to be my favorite spot, chatting all the while about her grandkids and the local goings-on that I had missed over the past five years. The seat feels familiar under me, the vinyl cool and slightly cracked. I slide in, taking a moment to look out at the main street, where the rhythm of life seems unchanged by time.

Martha hands me a menu, but I already know what I'll order—the same thing I always did. Meatloaf, home fries, green beans with bacon. Yet, I take the menu, if only to relive the ritual of tracing my fingers over the options, the descriptions of dishes that remind me of how my dad used to read them off to me when I was too young to so myself, swapping out real ingredients for outlandish ones.

Bug omelet. Fresh mashed skunk. Broccoli cheese casserole.

That last one was real, but it had horrified me as a small child as much as the thought of the other two.

"The usual, then?" Martha asks after a moment, her pen poised over her notepad. It surprises me, the warmth that floods my chest at being remembered.

"Yes, the usual sounds perfect," I say, handing back the menu. It feels like a reaffirmation of my ties to this place, to Granny's Kitchen, a staple of my childhood now welcoming me back as an old friend.

As Martha walks away, I lean back, letting the buzz of the diner wash over me. I'm no longer just a visitor passing through; I'm a piece of this town again, reweaving myself into its fabric. But there's undeniably a hole. The booth across from me is empty.

The wait for my meal passes quickly, filled with snippets of overheard conversations and the comforting routine of the diner. When my food arrives, it's exactly as I remember—simple, unpretentious, and utterly delicious. Eating alone, I'm surrounded by the ghosts of my past, but instead of feeling lonely, I'm enveloped in a sense of belonging. Granny's Kitchen hasn't just preserved its recipes; it's held onto pieces of every soul that's ever passed through its doors, mine included.

I savor my lunch, but little do I know, fate has more on the menu than just the daily special.

CHAPTER TWO: ETHAN

The bell above the diner door jingles its familiar greeting as I shoulder my way inside. The savory aroma of the grill and the murmur of midday conversation wrap around me like a well-worn jersey. I've got exactly forty-five minutes to inhale some fuel before practice, and then my next class and practice will demand every ounce of sweat and determination I can muster on the ice. Senior year, and I can almost taste the end of my college years. But the schedule, with hockey, is brutal sometimes.

"Hey, Ethan! Usual?" Martha, who has an uncanny memory for orders, calls out from behind the counter.

"Make it a double," I call back. My stomach growls in anticipation; the double burger is necessary. After all, defending the blue line doesn't come easy, and calories are just another form of ammunition.

Martha points to a booth, and I hustle toward it, but I'm busy scrolling through the latest stats on my phone. That's when it happens—a collision, the soft impact of someone barreling into me, followed by the clatter of plastic on tile.

"Shoot, sorry!"

I glance up, ready with an apology of my own, even though I hadn't moved an inch.

She's a flurry of motion, scrambling to pick up her phone, strands of chestnut hair falling across her face. It's Lily Morgan, the new sports marketer who's supposed to turn our team's luck around. The one who Marco got all aggro with this morning.

"Hey, no harm done." I hold up a hand and stoop to retrieve her phone from under the table. Her fingers brush mine as I hand it back, and those sharp green eyes lock onto mine. She's got that athletic stance—even frazzled and phoneless, she looks ready to take on a power play.

"Thanks." Her voice wobbles just a bit—embarrassment maybe? There's another spark there. Or am I imagining it? That's when I notice the phone case—a vintage-looking hockey rink layout that seems almost too fitting. They'd told us about her, and I vaguely recall that she used to play—in high school, was it? And she grew up here. I wouldn't have known her back then. My hometown is a much smaller town, Vallon, about two hours from Silverpeak. I'm a small-town boy just trying to make the best of his time in the city.

"Are you okay?" I ask, hoping my smile conveys enough warmth to counter any lingering embarrassment she might be feeling.

Lily blows out a breath, pushing back the hair that's fallen into her face. "Yeah, just trying to multitask and failing spectacularly at it. I was looking at my phone." She gives a self-deprecating grin that doesn't quite reach her eyes.

"Multitasking is overrated anyway," I quip, leaning casually against the nearest booth, aware of the curious glances from other diners. "And, confession, I was looking at my phone, too."

"Oh good," she says, tucking a strand of hair behind her ear. "I swear I'm not usually this clumsy." Her laugh is light, different from the intensity I remember from this morning's meeting. It makes my chest flutter just a little. Oh—yeah, Lily Morgan is definitely going to shake things up.

"First time for everything," I reply, trying not to sound too amused. "Nice to officially meet you," I add, offering her my hand. It's a firm shake—one that speaks of her confidence and drive. "Ethan Scott. Defenseman and evidently part-time phone retriever."

Her laughter is genuine this time, and I can't help but think how it brightens the entire room. "Well, Ethan Scott, thanks for rescuing my phone. The team really can't afford to lose any more players—or marketers—to silly accidents."

"Agreed." I nod, still holding onto her hand a second longer than necessary before letting go. "Maybe we should stick to our day jobs, huh?"

"Well, you seem to be taking on the job of constantly rescuing me. Thanks for stepping in earlier with Marco."

"I'm a peacemaker," I admit with a laugh. "But hey, it's all part of the welcome wagon here. And for the record, I'm really looking forward to working with you. And the others will come around." I mean it, too. Someone with her kind of energy is exactly what our team needs—someone to stir the pot and get us back on track.

Her athletic build seems to straighten with purpose, and I notice the way her eyes light up at the mention of work. "Thank you, Ethan. That means a lot, especially coming from you. I've researched your efforts off the ice. Volunteering, charity work—you're making quite the impact around here."

I feel a flicker of pride at her words. My family always instilled the importance of community in me, and it's something I take seriously. But right now, it's Lily's impressed gaze that's got my full attention. There's something about her earnestness, the way she doesn't shy away from giving credit where it's due—it's refreshing.

I fold my arms as I size up Lily's reaction. "It's no big deal," I say, playing down the acclaim with a half-smile. "Helping out is just part of who I am. My folks always said you get what you give, right? And we've got to look out for each other, in the rink and beyond." I shrug, hoping to convey modesty without brushing off her compliment entirely.

"Absolutely," she agrees, nodding. Her enthusiasm is contagious, and it's clear she's not the type to sit on the sidelines. With someone like Lily backing us, we might actually have a shot at turning things around. But before she can dig any deeper into my charity work, I steer us onto safer ice.

"Speaking of giving and getting," I start, sliding into my booth and gesturing to the seat across from me—which she takes. "The team's been on the receiving end of some rough press lately."

"Ah, yeah," Lily acknowledges, her tone turning serious, and her forehead creases with concern. "I've seen the headlines. Not exactly a marketer's dream, huh?"

"Definitely not." I let out a low chuckle, though there's nothing funny about our recent losing streak or the way the media's been eating us alive. It's like they smell blood in the water, and we're just circling sharks waiting for the next attack. Sponsors have bailed, and some of the guys who are on athletic scholarships are nervous.

"Office drama doesn't help either," I add, thinking about the last in-game scuffle that made it way too easily into the public eye. Or the last player busted for partying. Slipping grades. "But hey, that's where your marketing magic comes in, right?" I shoot her a playful wink.

"Magic?" She raises an eyebrow, a smile tugging at the corners of her lips. "You think I've got a wand hidden somewhere that'll fix all this?"

"Wouldn't surprise me at this point," I quip. The thought of Lily wielding a wand, conjuring up goodwill and positive spins, causes a genuine laugh to bubble up from my chest.

"Let's hope I won't need one," she says, her voice laced with the same humor. "I've got a few tricks up my sleeve, but it'll take some work from all of us. Even your reluctant friend, Marco."

"Whatever it takes to get us out of the penalty box with the public."

She studies me for a moment, and I wonder if she's looking for sincerity. I hope she finds it because I mean every word. Our team is more than just stats and scores; we're a family, and families stick together—through wins, losses, and terrible headlines.

"Good," she says finally, nodding with determination. "That's exactly what I wanted to hear."

Leaning back against the cool vinyl of the booth, I let the enthusiasm swell in my chest as I pitch an idea. "I've been brainstorming some community outreach programs. It's high time we got the locals rallying behind us again, you know? Like a charity match, or a 'Skate with the Team' day for kids."

Her eyes, those sharp green ones that seem to see right through the layers of someone, light up with interest. It's like watching the puck fly off a stick blade—fast and direct. "That sounds amazing, Ethan. I have something similar on my list of future plans."

"We could also set up hockey clinics. Teach the youngsters some skills, get them excited about the sport. Show that we're more than just players—we're role models."

She nods her approval. Martha shows up with a glass of iced tea for me, and Lily waves off anything else for herself. "I love it. And it's a perfect way to garner some good press." She props her elbows on the table, chin resting in her palms as she watches me, clearly considering the possibilities. "You really have given this a lot of thought."

"Can't stand idle when there's a challenge ahead," I say, the corner of my mouth quirking upward. The rink isn't the only place I play offense.

"Then maybe we should sit down sometime soon and hash out these plans properly?" Her suggestion, delivered with a tilt of her head and an earnest look, sends a jolt of something warm through me. Sparks, like skates kicking up ice shavings. I'm not sure if she's thinking anything other than professional-level, but my mind definitely goes there.

"Absolutely, I'd like that," I reply, maybe too quickly, but screw it—I'm not one to hide behind the boards when opportunity shoots my way. "There's plenty to discuss, and I reckon we make quite the team."

Her laugh, light and genuine, fills the space between us, and it's all I can do not to grin like an idiot who just scored the game-winning goal. "Well then, it's a date—a business date," she clarifies, but there's that playful glint in her eye that suggests she's not entirely opposed to the slip.

"Of course, purely professional," I assure her, though every fiber in my body is chanting for overtime. We're still in the first period here, but damn if I'm not looking forward to the rest of the game. "Let's make it official then," I say, fishing my phone out of the pocket of my jeans. "Your number?"

"Sure," Lily says with a quick nod, her shoulder-length hair swaying as she pulls out her own phone. Her fingers dance over the screen before she holds it out to me. "Here, I'll type mine in."

"Great reflexes," I tease, watching her enter her contact information.

"Comes with the territory," she replies, her green eyes meeting mine with that same competitive spark. It's clear she's not one to back down from a challenge, and neither am I.

"Got it," I confirm once her name is saved. "I'll send you a text so you have my number, too."

"Perfect." She pockets her phone.

As we sit there, a comfortable silence hovering, I realize this is more than just a professional exchange. There's an undercurrent of something else—maybe it's anticipation, or the beginning of teamwork beyond strategies and plays. My burger arrives, and Lily stands.

"I have to get back. But it was great chatting with you."

I stand too, nodding. "You, too. Should I see you out?"

"No, enjoy your food. See you around, Ethan." With a final nod, she heads toward the counter, leaving me with the echo of my name on her lips and the image of her soft, hurried smile.

Shaking my head, I settle back into the booth. Forty minutes to practice, and already the day feels like it's taken an unexpected turn. I watch her go, admiring the way she moves with purpose and grace. As she pushes open the door, sunlight frames her figure, casting her in a glow that seems to underscore everything I've just learned about her: passionate, driven, and undeniably beautiful.

I glance at the clock; practice is looming, but my mind's playing overtime with thoughts of Lily Morgan.

Lily Morgan. Huh.

She's not just another addition to the roster; Lily's got something that tells me she's going to leave a mark on this team, on this town. Maybe even on me.

I make short work of the double cheeseburger with the works, onion rings, and coleslaw. I have twenty-five minutes to go.

"Check, please," I call out to Martha, who nods and heads toward the register with a jingle of coins in her apron pocket.

As I stand, sliding into my well-worn leather jacket, the weight of my phone in the pocket feels like a promise. Maybe—if I'm lucky—a hint of something more personal, off the rink. I've always been good with a puck, but navigating this new chemistry? That's uncharted territory. I pay at the counter, my thoughts drifting.

"See ya, Ethan!" Martha waves as I head for the door.

"Thanks, catch you next time!" I toss back, already halfway out the door, the bell chiming my exit.

Outside, the air is crisp, biting at my cheeks and reminding me it's time to switch gears. Practice is calling, but it's not just drills and slap shots waiting for me—it's preparation for what comes after. For the first time in a long while, I'm itching to hit the books as much as the ice, to dive into strategies and plans that could change our game, all because Lily's passion has lit a fire under me.

I jog toward the rink, my breath visible in little clouds of ambition. Each stride pumps more adrenaline through my veins, fusing the excitement of potential plays with the image of Lily's green eyes and the easy confidence that seems to emanate from her every pore.

"Scott, you're looking pleased with yourself," Marco teases as I step into the locker room, his voice echoing off the walls. "Find a new deke move, or just happy to see us?"

"Maybe a bit of both," I shoot back with a grin, yanking open my locker. My gear greets me, familiar and ready, but today it feels like part of a bigger picture—one where hockey and heart might just go hand-in-hand. "You ready to hit the ice?"

An unreadable expression passes over his face. I notice he isn't in his gear, even though everyone else is already out on the rink.

"Nah," he says, fidgeting with his phone absently. "I'm sitting this one out. I'm in time-out, you could say."

"Silv," I chide. Not again. "What now?"

He shrugs. "Nothing as bad as I've ever done, but worse than you would do."

I sigh. I have to get out there, but I want to stay and lecture Marco about his partying—he's a big influence on the other players, and if he changed his ways, maybe Lily wouldn't have such an uphill battle on her hands.

“Plus side, I get a little one-on-one with the new marketing bit after practice, so maybe it’ll be worth it.”

Something about his flippant tone makes me bristle inside. I say nothing, just slam my locker closed and leave the locker room. As I suit up, I replay the morning's chance encounter. There's an energy there that goes beyond the ice, something that tells me Lily and I are going to make one hell of a team. And as I strap on my skates, ready to carve up the rink, I know that this is just the pre-game warm-up.

As I step onto the ice, the chill beneath my blades a welcome thrill. My mind is racing faster than a breakaway—filled with plays and possibilities, schemes and dreams, and the undeniable pleasant flutter that comes with new attraction. Practice may be about discipline and teamwork, but right now, I’m skating on potential—and it’s a rush.

CHAPTER THREE: MARCO

I'm slumped in the bleachers, the cold metal seeping through my jeans and into my skin, but it's a numbness I deserve. The empty rink echoes with the ghost of last night's mistakes—a cacophony of laughter, clinking glasses, and too many toasts that had no reason behind them except to dull the sting of the last game's defeat. My head is pounding, and so is the guilt. Each reveler's face is a snapshot of another PR disaster I've single-handedly served up on a silver platter. Social media is brutal, but I guess if you never get photographed blind drunk outside a bar, they won't have fuel.

"Wild Shot" Silvestri they call me, but last night's antics were anything but calculated. Every article or post branding me as the team's reckless party boy feels like a puck to the gut. The management isn't amused, the Dean isn't amused, the coaches—you get the idea. And neither am I. And now there's Lily—the PR cleanup crew summoned to mop up my mess. The thought grates on me; another person trying to put Marco Silvestri in a box. But what kills me is that she'll probably succeed, and it'll be a feather in her just-arrived-on-scene cap.

The sound of the door swinging open breaks my reverie, and I look down from my perch. She strides in—Lily Morgan. It's clear from her walk alone she knows her way around a hockey rink. There's purpose in her steps, and I begrudgingly admire that. Her athletic build is outlined by fitted jeans and a jacket that does nothing to hide the fact that she's no stranger to sports. Or discipline. Or, apparently, turning a total screw-up like myself into a presentable human being. Because I know that a whole mess of people are tired of me being, well, a mess.

Her chestnut hair bounces with each step she takes onto the ice, standing out against the pristine white surface. Those green eyes are scanning the arena, missing nothing, and somehow, I know before they even land on me that I'm about to be dissected, analyzed, and reassembled into something more palatable for public consumption. I lean down and tug at my skate laces.

I push off the bleacher, standing tall. She hasn't looked up at me yet, but she will. They always do. Maybe it's the height, or maybe it's the reputation that precedes me. Women love a bad boy. But this woman is a professional bad-boy tamer, so will she fall for it? I'm Marco Silvestri, after all. Not that it matters if she does—women are a dime a dozen in my world.

Either way, my annoyance simmers. She's here to fix me, but I'm not some strategy you can scribble on a whiteboard. I play hard on the ice and off. No apologies, no regrets.

Until now, apparently.

As she comes closer, clipboard in hand like a shield, I steel myself for the onslaught of charm and disarming humor. They say she's good, but I wonder if she's ready for the likes of me. Because despite the mess I've made, one thing's for sure—I won't go down without a fight.

"Miss Morgan," I begin, my voice echoing through the empty arena, "I hope you've brought your magic wand because it's going to take more than a sprinkle of fairy dust to clean up this mess."

Her gaze lifts from the clipboard, locking on to mine with an unflappable steadiness that catches me off guard. She frowns slightly when I say *magic wand.* She's not swayed by the charm that has others melting like ice in the sun. Annoyingly intriguing.

"Mr. Silvestri," she responds coolly, her voice steady, stopping mid-rink. "If you're looking for miracles, I suggest a church. What I bring is a strategy, but it requires something you might not be familiar with—accountability."

Her words are a slapshot to my ego, and I feel the smirk that dances on my lips. She's got guts—I'll give her that. But she's playing in the big leagues now, and I'm the MVP of hard-to-handle.

"Accountability?" I echo mockingly, leaning casually against the edge of the rink wall. "I score goals, Miss Morgan, not good-boy points. The press loves drama; they eat it up. So what if I give them a little show?" I come out onto the ice, pushing off the boards.

Lily steps closer, and I can see the fire in her eyes now. She's not just here to do a job; she's here to make a difference. It's disconcerting, the way it makes me want to actually listen.

"Your 'show' affects more than just you," she counters sharply, "The team, the fans, the kids who look up to you. The school itself—you're making it harder for anyone coming after you to be thought of as an upright citizen. You're reinforcing the party-boy college stereotype. You have talent, Marco, but you're squandering it under the spotlight of the wrong kind of fame."

She's got me there. I know she's right, the team doesn't need another headline of Wild Shot Silvestri's wild nights out. Still, it's easier to keep up the façade than to admit the chaos it's causing. But as Lily stands there, unrelenting, I feel something shift—a twinge of respect, maybe even the urge to be better.

"Fine," I relent, just a little, digging my blades in to circle around her. "Say I buy into this plan of yours. What's step one? Apology tour? Community service? Or do we jump straight to knitting sweaters for orphaned puppies?"

Her laugh surprises me, light and genuine, and it chips away at the wall I've built up. For a second, I let myself imagine what it would be like to be on her side, fighting for something instead of always pushing back. It's disconcerting. I've spent nearly the last four years making myself infamous

"Step one," Lily says, her smile lingering, "is realizing that this isn't a game. It's real life, and it's time you start playing it with the same commitment you show on the ice."

She's calling me out, challenging me in a way no one has dared before. And damn if it doesn't make me want to rise to the occasion. When she looks at me with those challenging eyes, I can't resist throwing a little sass back her way.

"Well, I don't see you scoring any goals. So maybe you should just focus on damage control?"

"I only see *your* success in the rink," she snaps back, clearly trying to get a rise out of me.

I smirk, leaning back against the boards, my arms folded across my chest. "I score wherever I play, Morgan. But let's hear this master plan of yours," I shoot back, curious despite myself.

"First," she begins, all confident and business-like, "no more nightlife escapades splashed across social media. We're going blackout on that front."

"Blackout? That's rich. You want me to be hermit?" I can't help but chuckle.

"Seriously, Marco, it's time to show your fans a side of you that doesn't end with a hangover."

"Fans love a bad boy," I counter, unable to resist flirting with danger, even in conversation.

"Sure, until the bad boy fumbles the puck because he's too hungover to see straight," she counters, light but firm.

"Ouch," I laugh. She's got guts, I'll give her that. "You don't pull any punches, do you?"

"Never had the luxury," she fires back, then dives into step two of her grand plan: making me the face of charity events and youth hockey clinics.

"You really think you can just waltz in here and fix everything with a couple of interviews and some staged photo ops?" I ask, the skepticism heavy in my tone. "Who says I want to show people anything? Maybe I like my life just the way it is." My arms cross over my chest defensively.

"Because it's not just about you," she fires back. "You're part of a team, remember? Your actions affect everyone—your teammates, the fans, the kids who look up to you."

"Kids don't look up to me," I mutter, but even as I say it, I know it's a lie. I've seen the way they cheer when I take to the ice, how their faces light up when I score. It's a rush, but it's also a responsibility—one I've been ignoring for too long.

"Maybe they should," Lily says softly, and I can't tell if it's a challenge or an encouragement. "Being a part of this team means being a role model, whether you like it or not. You have the chance to make a real difference, Marco. Don't waste it."

I'm silent for a moment, torn between irritation and a grudging respect. The truth is, I don't do well with authority, but Lily...she isn't like any PR flack I've met before. She believes in this stuff, believes in me, which is throwing me.

"You think I'm role model material?" I can't hide my skepticism, but deep down, I'm a little intrigued.

"Everyone has potential," she insists. "Even you, Silvestri. It's about leveraging your charm for good. Besides, it'll be good press."

"Charm?" I lean in, teasing her. "Didn't realize you were so taken by it."

"Professional observation," she retorts, not taking the bait. Then she's on about rebuilding my image with candid interviews, showing off a side of me that isn't just about the mischief.

I circle her again, silent, thinking. "I'm telling you right now that I'm not known as a Boy Scout around here."

She spins on her heel to face me. "That's true. You've got one hell of a reputation for lighting up the nightlife as much as you do the ice. It might not be ideal as a rep, but it's not worthless either."

Curiosity piques within me, despite the ego that tells me to shut this down. "What are you getting at?"

"We can use it," she says simply, eyes alight with a kind of excitement that's hard to ignore. "We can show this city there's more to Marco Silvestri than wild parties and tabloid headlines. Let's organize a charity event—something high-profile and glamorous, sure, but for a good cause. Show the public the man who plays for the love of the game, who cares about something bigger than himself."

"Charity gala?" I repeat, skepticism lacing my tone even as the notion tugs at something inside me. "You think putting on a suit and smiling for cameras will change what people think of me?"

"Only if the suit fits and the smile is genuine," she counters with a smirk. "People love a bad boy, but they go crazy for a bad boy with a heart of gold."

I scoff, but her words echo in my head, stirring a mix of annoyance and... intrigue? It's been a while since someone looked at me and saw potential rather than problems. "So, what, we throw a party with a purpose, and suddenly I'm the prodigal son? You think the NHL is looking for a redemption story when they scout?"

"Proving yourself isn't about perfection or some kind of con on the way to stardom, Marco," she says, stepping closer. "It's about effort. The community wants to forgive you, they just need to see you're more than your mistakes."

"Sounds like you've got it all figured out," I say, feeling strangely lighter, maybe even a bit hopeful about this whole thing.

"Trust me, I'm just getting started," she says with that determined look in her eye. "Are you in, or am I wasting my time?"

"Well, I'm one hangover from a suspension, so I guess we'll find out, won't we?" I reply, feeling resigned.

"Guess we will," she agrees. "but it's you they need to see. Are you ready to step up, or is Wild Shot all talk?"

For a moment, there's a standstill. My pride wars with the part of me that's sick of being the punchline, and in the end, it's her drive that tips the scales. Lily Morgan doesn't know it yet, but she's got me considering the play. Maybe this spitfire has a point, and maybe, just maybe, I'm ready to see where this goes. But as I watch her, all athletic poise and no-nonsense attitude, I feel like a rat in a trap.

"Fine," I sigh, running a hand through my hair. "We'll do it your way. But if this blows up in my face, it's on you."

"Deal," she agrees, and there's a spark in her eye that tells me she loves a challenge.

"What's your first move, Coach?"

A triumphant smile plays at the corner of her lips. "First, we start with some community service. Easy stuff. You'll help out at a local youth hockey clinic. "

"Ah, community service," I say, scratching the back of my head. "Because nothing says 'reformed party boy' like slapping on a pair of skates and pretending to care, right?"

"Who says you have to pretend?" she retorts, crossing her arms. There's a challenge in her tone that sets my competitive edge ablaze. "You might even enjoy it." She steps toward me, closing the distance between us. "Trust me."

And as I look down into those fiery green eyes, I'm surprised to find a part of me that actually does. Without warning, her hand reaches out, her fingers brushing lightly against mine. It's brief, accidental, maybe, but it sends a jolt of electricity racing through me. For a heartbeat, the world falls silent, and all I can see is her—Lily Morgan, the woman who might just be the game-changer I never knew I needed.

“I, uh. I do.”

"Good," she whispers, her breath a warm whisper.

"Good," I echo, and as she turns away, the ghost of her touch lingers, leaving me wondering what the hell just happened. For a guy who's spent his life dodging anything resembling real connection, I'm suddenly, inexplicably, looking forward to our next play.

As we turn to leave the rink, I catch a glimpse of myself in the glass, my reflection superimposed over the empty stands. For the first time in a long time, I'm not sure what I see looking back at me. But maybe, just maybe, Lily Morgan can help me figure it out.

CHAPTER FOUR: LILY

The cool darkness of the pre-dawn office is nothing like the turmoil that's been churning in my mind all night. I unlock the door and step inside, flicking on the lights and taking a deep breath. Yesterday's PR disaster looms over me like a storm cloud, but I'm Lily Morgan; I don't cower from storms—I chase them.

I dump my bag on my desk—a cluttered illustration of my nonstop work ethic—and head straight for the kitchenette. The quiet hum of the refrigerator greets me as I grab a coffee pod and slam it into the machine. It's going to take more than a good slap shot to get through today, it's going to take a whole lot of caffeine.

As the coffee pours, rich and dark, into my mug, I can't think about the community rink on the east side of town—how the cold air would bite at my cheeks and how Dad would say, "Lils, you gotta play the puck where it lies." The ice may be different here, but the game's the same. Time to play it.

Cradling my steaming cup of motivation, I shuffle back to my desk, snagging a pastry from the box I picked up on my way in. Chocolate croissant—breakfast of champions and desperate sports marketing directors. I sink into my chair, the leather creaking under the weight of impending decisions.

"Okay, Lily," I mutter to myself, "think outside the box."

Pen tapping against my lips, I start scribbling down ideas, all while taking generous bites of the buttery pastry. Community outreach programs, charity matches, fan meet-and-greets... But they all feel like rehashed plays from an old playbook.

"Needs to be fresh, something no one sees coming," I say, brushing off the crumbs. If there's one thing growing up in a hockey-centric town has taught me, it's that the most effective strategies often come from the element of surprise. I lean back, eyes scanning the whiteboard across the room littered with strategies and motivational quotes.

The negative press won't just clear out like fog after a morning skate—it requires strategy, finesse, and maybe, just maybe, a wild card that no one expects. And I'm not sure if a few photo-ops with kids will reform the image of Wild Shot Marco.

I gulp down the last of my coffee, feeling it embolden my veins with warmth and a spike of energy. As I pace the length of my office, each step is a metronome to the brainstorming symphony in my head. Ideas float like puck on ice but none grip hard enough for the shot. Then, it hits me—the slapshot idea that's so bold it might just ricochet into brilliance.

My green eyes fixate on the whiteboard, narrowing with determination. The team's image is on thin ice, but I'm not one to shy away from a challenge. With every sip and every thought, the edges of a daring plan begin to crystallize, forming into something that might just be crazy enough to work.

Marco, who takes home a new coed every night, and isn't shy about kissing and telling. It's his level of respect—or disrespect—that is part of our problem.

But what if he was suddenly a one-woman man?

"Stage a relationship... with Marco?" The words dribble out before I can stick-handle them back into silence. Me and Marco? It's ludicrous, sure, but as the team's marketer, I'm desperate to pull us out of this PR nosedive. And who better to concoct a love story with than the most talked-about player on—and off—the ice?

"Wild Shot" Silvestri has the charm and the headlines to flip our narrative. With a deep breath that does nothing to steady my racing heart, I snag my phone and text him, thankful that we'd exchanged numbers before parting the prior afternoon.

Where are you?

On the ice, he replies a few moments later. *Missed practice yesterday, remember?*

I make my way to the rink. My sneakers squeak against the polished floors, echoing in the vast, empty arena. Morning light filters through the high windows, casting long shadows over the benches where Marco often sits. But they're empty.

"Marco?" My voice carries across the ice as I spot him practicing shots, alone, his focus complete. I know he's more than tabloid fodder; beneath that party-boy veneer is a dedicated athlete with a sharp mind. Now, it's time to tap into that potential.

"Hey, Lily!" Marco calls out, his voice bouncing off the walls. His dark hair is tousled from his helmet, sticking to his olive skin, and those deep brown eyes squint as he smiles, pushing away any lingering hesitation I have. "What brings you down here so early?"

"Strategy," I say, stepping onto the bench to bridge the distance between safety and the gamble I'm about to take. "And you're part of it."

"Am I now?" He crosses his arms, leaning on his hockey stick with a look that's all too mischievous. This is typical Marco, always ready to dance along the edge.

"Big part." I take another step, the chill from the ice creeping up through my soles. "I want us to pretend we're dating."

"Come again?" He blinks, and for a brief moment, the swagger subsides, exposing a flicker of vulnerability.

"Fake it 'til we make it, Silvestri," I continue, channeling every ounce of confidence I have. "The team's image needs a makeover, and what better way than a heartwarming romance to steer the conversation? You and I could be the feel-good story of the season."

He looks at me, studying my face as if he might find the punchline etched into my skin. But there's no joke to be found—only the serious proposal of a woman backed into a corner by circumstance and armed with a Hail Mary play.

"Isn't that a bit drastic?" He finally smirks, but I can tell he's intrigued.

"Drastic times," I quip, meeting his gaze squarely. "You've got the bad-boy rep, I've got the good-girl charm. Together, we can spin this into gold. We just need to convince the fans and the press that we're the real deal."

"Acting like a couple to save the team, huh?" He shifts, tapping his stick against his skate in a rhythmic beat. "Sounds like something straight out of a romcom."

"Listen, Marco," I stress—with more confidence than I feel—"I know the idea sounds unconventional, but it's got legs. Authenticity is key in sports marketing these days. Fans want a story they can believe in."

Marco leans back, his arms crossed over his chest, an amused expression playing on his lips. "You're saying we pretend to date, and everyone just buys it? You do realize I'm not exactly Prince Charming to these people?"

"Which is precisely why this will work." I lean forward, my hands animatedly sketching out the vision. "It's redemption, transformation! Your image does a 180 because of love. It's the kind of narrative that gets people talking—for the right reasons."

He raises an eyebrow, the corner of his mouth twitching. "And you think you can pull off being madly in love with me, eh?"

The challenge in his tone sparks a fire in me. "I was head of the drama club in high school, thank you very much. Besides," I say, winking at him, "it's all about good PR. And I've got connections."

"Connections?" His interest piques, dark eyes locking onto mine.

"Childhood friend turned editor at 'Heartbeat Magazine.' We get featured in the next issue, and voila, instant buzz. The story will be that I came to town for the job because of you. My influence calms the notorious Wild Shot."

He runs a hand through his tousled hair, considering my words. "That's... actually not the worst idea you've had."

"Thank you, I'll choose to take that as a compliment." I flash him a grin, sensing victory. I smile, tapping into our shared sense of humor. "So, what do you say, Wild Shot? Are you in, or are you benched?"

Marco pauses, the weight of the decision hanging between us like a puck suspended mid-air, and then, with a grin that lights up his whole face, he makes the pass. "Alright, Morgan. Let's give them a show they won't forget. But if we're doing this, it has to look good. Really good."

"Agreed." I nod enthusiastically. "There's a place by the lake, trees, open sky. It's picturesque—the perfect spot to sell our 'romance.'"

"Outdoor shoot, huh?" He smirks, standing up. "Better make sure they catch my good side."

"Right now, no sides are your good side, remember?" Deep down, there's a flutter of something other than nerves at the thought of staging intimacy with Marco. I push it aside. This is business.

"Right," he chuckles.

"I'm going to make the call," I say, already jogging backward and turning to sprint back to my office, calling over my shoulder. "Are you free this afternoon?"

"For you, dearest, I can be," he replies, vamping. "Just text me when and where, pookie!"

I roll my eyes—this is either the best idea I've ever had, or it's about to be my biggest disaster. But if hockey has taught me anything, it's that sometimes you have to take the shot—even when the net seems miles away.

***

The camera sits perched atop its tripod like a hawk, waiting for the perfect moment to swoop down. I adjust myself in front of the lens, angling toward the spot where the morning sun spills across the lakeshore, painting everything with a golden glow. We've snagged our feature, but the magazine can't spare a photographer today—so I've taken matters into my own hands. A few quick calls, and the college's photography department generously loaned me all I needed.

This has to work.

"Looking good, honeybuns." The voice is teasing, rife with that familiar Italian intonation that can send a shiver down my spine.

I spin around to find Marco sauntering toward me, fashionably late as promised—or perhaps as expected. He's wearing a fitted white T-shirt that does nothing to hide the contours of his athletic build, and jeans that look like they've been molded to his legs. Confidence rolls off him in waves, and despite the irritation at his punctuality, or lack thereof, I can't deny the flutter in my stomach when our eyes meet.

"Try 'punctual' sometime. It's all the rage," I quip, checking my watch, though I'm fully aware that he's well within the time frame of 'fashionably late.'

He grins, a full display of mischief in those deep brown eyes. "You started without me?"

"Someone had to make sure this looked believable," I retort, gesturing at the meticulously arranged picnic blanket, complete with a strategically placed basket and a couple of wine glasses waiting to be filled with sparkling cider.

"Ah, romance by the book. How quaint." Marco picks up one of the glasses, inspecting it with feigned scrutiny.

"Quaint is what sells magazines, Silvestri." I snatch the glass from him before he can smudge it with fingerprints. "And it's your job to sell it."

"Is it?" He steps closer, and I'm suddenly very aware of how much space he occupies—how much heat he radiates.

"Absolutely," I say, standing my ground with hands on hips. "Remember, you're the reformed bad boy. Show me some of that hidden vulnerability."

"Hidden, huh?" His smirk grows, and he leans in just a fraction too close, his voice lowering. "Let's not forget who needs who in this little charade, Morgan."

"Trust me, I haven't forgotten. I'm just waiting for you to show your appreciation." Our banter could cut through ice, and right now, I'm skating on thin layers, trying to keep my composure.

"Really?" Marco steps even closer up, rolling his shoulders back in a way that seems both casual and calculated. I feel my cheeks heat.

"Let's get this show on the road then, shall we?" I step away, heart pounding a little harder than I'd like to admit. “William?”

A few yards away is William, who is also on loan from the arts department. He's a freshman, and a little shy, but I have no idea what all the buttons and lenses on the very expensive camera do, and so William was obliged to come along.

As he picks up the remote for the camera, I remind myself that this is just strategy, a play we have to execute perfectly. "Wild Shot" Silvestri may be unpredictable on the ice, but here, in this contrived scene of romantic bliss, I'm the one calling the shots. At least, that's what I keep telling myself.

Soon, the camera clicks and whirs, a mechanical heartbeat in the stillness of the outdoor setting. I'm standing way too close to Marco, our sides almost touching, trying to hold a pose that screams "couple" without screaming "awkward" even louder. But who am I kidding? The tension is as palpable as the crisp air nipping at our skin.

"Chin up, Lily," William directs, his voice patient but strained. I comply, tilting my head ever so slightly, seeking an angle that doesn't make me look like a deer in headlights.

"Feels like we're posing for one of those cheesy romance novel covers, doesn't it?" I venture, aiming for humor to bridge the gap between us. My words hang in the air, waiting for Marco's volley.

"Except you forgot the part where the shirtless guy with flowing locks sweeps you off your feet," Marco quips back, a lopsided grin tugging at one corner of his mouth.

"Right, how could I forget the mandatory wind machine and the Fabio hair," I say, rolling my eyes, hoping my smile looks more amused than pained. He chuckles, the sound warm but fleeting.

"Okay, now look into each other's eyes," William instructs, breaking into our stilted attempt at banter. We do as told, and I'm suddenly lost in the deep brown pools of Marco's eyes. They're like dark chocolate, rich and forbidden, and for a moment, I forget why we're here. But then reality buzzes in my ear like a pesky mosquito. “Imagine something you love…”

"Yeah, Lil. Imagine I just scored the winning goal, and you're so proud you can't help but..." Marco starts, his voice a low murmur meant just for me.

"Jump into your arms and plant one on you?" I offer, my tone dripping with sarcasm, but inside, my stomach does a traitorous little flip.

"Exactly," he says, the edges of his eyes crinkling with amusement. "Now you're getting it."

I resist the urge to roll my eyes again. Instead, I plaster on the brightest, most convincing smile I can muster, as if I truly believe in this facade we're constructing. The camera clicks away, immortalizing our pretend love story one awkward frame at a time.

"Let's try something else to loosen up," William suggests. I can tell he's trying to make magic out of a mess. We've been at this for what feels like hours, shifting from one stereotypical lovey-dovey pose to another under the keen eye of his lens. "Tell me about your first hockey game, Marco. The real experience, not the press release version."

Marco hesitates for a fraction of a second before launching into the tale, and I listen, genuinely interested. As he talks, his body relaxes, and I find myself watching him, drawn in by the passion in his voice. This is the side of him I need the world to see—the thoughtful, dedicated athlete with dreams bigger than any tabloid scandal.

And for a moment, just a brief, shining moment, we find our rhythm.

"Marco, pull her close, and Lily, just look up at him, like you're lost in his eyes."

I scooch closer to Marco, feeling the solid warmth of his arm as it wraps around my waist, almost protective. I tilt my head up to meet his gaze, those deep brown eyes that seem to hold stories untold. But instead of a spark, all I see is a mirror of my own discomfort—the previous ease completely gone.

"Smile, Lily!" William calls out.

I stretch my lips into what must be the fakest smile ever plastered on a human face. The camera clicks repeatedly, capturing every cringe-worthy moment. I can sense Marco's muscles tense beneath his shirt—the same tension I'm holding in my core—as we both play our parts in this clumsy dance.

We shift again, this time with me standing behind him, my arms looped loosely around his neck. It's an intimate pose—one that should feel natural, easy even—but there's nothing easy about pretending to adore someone you barely know. Especially when that someone is Marco Silvestri, the Silverpeak Sabres' biggest bad boy and your ticket to salvaging a sinking ship.

"Beautiful! Now, Marco, look over your shoulder at her—yeah, like that!"

I can practically hear William's desperation to get one decent shot out of this debacle. He moves around us, snapping photos from every angle imaginable, but each click feels like glass breaking in the hollow space between us.

"Okay, last one," he finally announces, and relief floods through me. We've been twisting ourselves into romantic pretzels for too long, and the act is wearing thin.

"Let's end with a forehead touch. Really sell it, you two."

Our heads come together, and for a second, our eyes lock. There's a flicker of...something, a silent conversation in a shared glance. Disappointment. Frustration. Maybe even a mutual understanding that we're in over our heads. Our foreheads press against each other, a forced symbol of closeness that feels anything but close.

"Got it. Thanks, you two," William says, though his tone lacks conviction.

As we break apart, the physical distance we put between ourselves is nothing compared to the emotional miles we still have to cross. We need to do better; we need to be better—at this charade, at understanding each other.

"Sorry," Marco mumbles, running a hand through his tousled hair. "I'm not much of an actor."

"Neither am I," I admit, tucking a stray chestnut strand behind my ear. "I was in drama, but I mostly built sets. But we have to make this work, Marco. The team needs it."

He nods, the corners of his mouth twitching upward in a half-hearted attempt at a reassuring smile. We're partners in this bizarre ruse, whether we like it or not.

"Come on," I say, a plan already forming in my mind. "Let's grab some coffee and figure out our next move. We can't fool anyone if we can't even fool ourselves."

"Thanks for your patience today," I say to the photographer, offering a bright smile that doesn't quite reach my eyes. "I'm sure we've got some excellent shots in there."

William packs up his gear with a nod, his expression polite but noncommittal. The poor guy had tried everything, from telling jokes to suggesting increasingly ridiculous poses to coax some semblance of real emotion out of us. But as he slings his camera bag over his shoulder and waves goodbye, I can tell he's not holding his breath.

"See you next time," I call out after him, the words tasting like a promise I'm not sure I can keep.

Marco watches the photographer leave. "Think he bought it?" His voice is laced with that characteristic blend of sarcasm and charm that usually annoys me—usually.

"Let's just say he's good at hiding his skepticism." I sigh, glancing down at my own hands. They're still slightly shaky from trying too hard to appear casually intertwined with Marco's during the shoot.

"Next time, huh?" Marco pushes off from the railing and steps closer. There's a hint of real curiosity behind his teasing tone now. "You really think there'll be a next time?"

"Of course," I say with more conviction than I feel. "Practice makes perfect."

"Or perfectly awkward," he quips, but the smirk on his face doesn't quite mask the concern in his deep brown eyes. But then, his hand on my arm snaps me back to reality. "We'll figure it out. You're the brains of the operation, right?"

"Right," I affirm, though it feels like I'm trying to convince myself more than him.

"Good. Because I'm starving, and I can't think on an empty stomach." He grins, and for a moment, the humor reaches his eyes, giving me a glimpse of the genuine connection I'm desperate to create.

"Food," I echo, grateful for the change of subject. "Lead the way, Wild Shot."

We part ways at the edge of the park, agreeing to meet at a nearby diner. As I walk alone, the chill in the air isn't enough to stop the heat of frustration that burns in my cheeks. This has to work. For the team, for my career... maybe even for something more personal than I'm ready to admit.

The thought of crafting a lie so elaborate it becomes truth is daunting. Yet, as I rehearse potential scenarios in my head, a stubborn resolve takes root. I have to make this work, no matter how many staged kisses and artificial embraces it takes. No matter how much I have to push through the awkwardness and bridge the gap between pretense and something real. I can't lose this job, my first out of school. And I know Marco doesn't want to lose his spot on the Sabres or get kicked out of school so late in the game.

Because somewhere between those forced smiles and staged touches, there's a spark waiting to ignite. And I, Lily Morgan, am determined to fan it into a flame.

As I get into my car, my phone dings. It's Ethan.

What were the cross streets, again?

Crap. I forgot that I our first player outreach was this afternoon. Things were moving so fast. I had to be at the park on the opposite side of town in—I check the clock—an hour.

I text Marco apologies, and promise to coordinate another meetup soon. He texts back: *No problem, baby. Just say the word, and I'll drop everything for you.*

Then, he has the stones to add a kiss-face emoji.

Just to get under my skin.

I ignore him and put the car into gear after sending Ethan a pin that will help him map his way to the park. I'm already losing track, getting scattered. It's time to refocus.

CHAPTER FIVE: ETHAN

I pull up to the community center, feeling rushed after class. I step out of my car and head toward the bustle of activity that has already started without me. Lily is at the heart of it all, directing volunteers with the ease of a seasoned conductor leading an orchestra. She's in her element here, shoulder-length shiny hair tied back into a functional ponytail, green eyes scanning the area for anything amiss. Her voice carries over the chatter, clear and commanding, yet there's a warmth there that makes you want to listen, to be part of whatever she's building.

"Hey, Ethan!" Lily calls out, catching sight of me as I approach. Her smile is like a break in the clouds, brightening the grey day. I've wanted to text her—a lot—since we'd exchanged numbers, but I've refrained except for professional matters.

"Hey, Lily," I reply, returning her smile with one of my own. I'm not used to being out and about unless it's for class or practice lately, but seeing her so energized gives me a jolt that no amount of coffee could match.

"Thanks for coming. Let me introduce you to everyone," she says, looping her arm through mine in a friendly gesture that somehow sends a spark up my spine. She leads me around, introducing me to the team of volunteers who've gathered. They're a mix of ages and backgrounds, but they all share a look of determination that I recognize from my own team locker room before a big game.

"Everyone, this is Ethan Scott, defenseman for our very own hockey team." Lily's introduction comes with an emphasis that makes me stand a little taller. "We're here not just to revitalize this old park, but to show the community that The Sabres are more than what happens on the ice."

She talks about the importance of giving back, of being part of something larger than ourselves, and I find myself nodding along. It's easy to forget sometimes, amidst the grueling schedule and the pressure to win, that there's a world outside the rink that needs us too.

"Let's show them what teamwork really looks like," she finishes, and there's a chorus of agreement that ripples through the group. I'm handed a pair of work gloves and a shovel.

My gloves feel awkwardly bulky as I shove them into my pockets, suddenly aware of the *metaphorical* stick in my hand—this project, this chance to do some good. It's a different kind of game, but the objective is the same: work together, support each other, and aim for victory.

"Ready to get your hands dirty?" Lily asks, her tone teasing but her eyes serious. There's a challenge there, and I've never been one to back down from a challenge.

"Absolutely," I say, the word firm and decisive.

The volunteers cheer, a sound that is surprisingly invigorating, and I feel an unexpected surge of pride. This is more than just a photo op or a PR stunt—it's about making a real difference, and I'm starting to see just how much that matters to Lily.

For the next hour, I shovel mulch onto the flower beds, trying to wrap my head around this whole community outreach thing. Sure, I grew up learning the value of giving back, but can we really change how people see us with a few shovelfuls of dirt? Lily seems to think so, and I'm finding it hard not to get caught up in her enthusiasm. There's something about the way she rallies everyone, her green eyes sparking with purpose.

Lily comes over, and I'm overly aware once again.

"Hey, Ethan, you're doing great, but let me show you a trick to make it spread more evenly," Lily says, approaching me with that athletic grace of hers. She takes the shovel from my hands, and for a moment, our fingers brush against each other. A jolt of electricity shoots through me, unexpected and not entirely unwelcome.

"Like this," she demonstrates, her movements efficient and precise. "You want to create a gentle slope away from the plant base to help with water drainage."

"Got it, coach," I reply, taking back the shovel. It feels warmer somehow, like it's been charged by her touch. "Thanks for the pro tip."

"Anytime." She winks, then moves on to check in with the other volunteers.

I follow her instructions, smoothing out the mulch as she showed me. The motion is rhythmic, almost soothing, and I fall into a steady pace. I steal glances at Lily as she works alongside the others, her hair catching stray beams of sunlight despite the overcast sky.

She catches me looking and grins, a mischievous twinkle in her eye. "Keep your eyes on your own mulch, Scott."

"Can't help it if there's a better view elsewhere," I shoot back, and she laughs, a light, genuine sound that makes me want to hear it again.

"Flattery will get you everywhere," she teases, then promptly trips over a garden hose hidden beneath a pile of leaves.

"Whoa!" I lunge forward to steady her, and for a second, once I catch her, we're closer than we've been all day. Her breath fans across my face, smelling faintly of peppermint and coffee, and I suddenly wish we were anywhere but here, surrounded by volunteers and bags of soil.

"Thanks," she says, her voice slightly breathless as she regains her balance. "Guess I need to keep my eyes on my own... hoses."

"Guess so," I manage to respond, though my voice sounds rough even to my own ears. My hand still rests on her arm, and I can feel the firmness of her muscle beneath her jacket. This girl is no delicate flower; she's as tough as any hockey player I've known.

"Back to work?" she suggests, stepping back with a rueful smile.

"Back to work," I echo, reluctantly letting go.

We resume our tasks, the easy banter continuing between us. It's dangerous territory, this flirtatious game we're playing. I can't afford distractions—not with the team depending on me, my last few classes in the mix—but Lily Morgan is proving to be one hell of a distraction. And I'm not sure how long I'll want to resist.

We move next to shelving for the maintenance shed at the park, and I'm overjoyed that she snags me as a work partner.

"Hand me that hammer, will you?" Lily asks without taking her eyes off the half-built shelving unit in front of us. She's all focus and drive, and it's pretty damn impressive.

"Sure thing, boss," I say, passing her the tool. There's warmth in the way she smiles at me—like we're in on a joke nobody else gets.

"Ever done anything like this before?" I ask as I hold a plank steady for her. Her swing is confident, sure—a mirror to her personality.

"Built an entire set of bleachers for my high school's baseball field once," she says with a proud tilt of her chin. "Took forever, but it was worth it. You?"

"Helped renovate a community center back in high school. Painted a mural, too. My stick figure art was the talk of the town." I grin, hoping to earn another one of her laughs.

"Jack of all trades, huh?" She doesn't disappoint, her laughter ringing clear and bright.

"Master of none," I counter, feeling a camaraderie building between us that's about more than just the project at hand.

We move on to another section, and talk shifts to the team. "How are you handling Marco's latest escapade?" I can't avoid asking. Every guy on the team has been sweating the fallout.

"Marco's... a handful," she admits, but her tone is light, not giving away much. "But I've got a few ideas up my sleeve. Don't worry, I'll keep him in line."

I nod, appreciating her confidence, even though part of me wants to dig deeper—there's something she's not saying. But I let it slide. For now.

"Hey, Ethan!" A voice calls out, pulling my attention away. It's one of the volunteers pointing to the sky. Dark clouds have been gathering, and as if on cue, a cold gust of wind barrels through, sending a stack of flyers flying—another of her ideas, contact info for the team's new "outreach" initiative.

"Whoa!" Lily catches a runaway sheet as it flutters past her face. I'm right behind her, grabbing what I can. Our efforts turn into a sort of dance, chasing after the whims of the wind, laughter mingling with the sound of rustling paper.

"Nice catch!" I commend as she pins a flyer against a tree with swift precision.

"Thanks! You're not so bad yourself," she retorts, a playful glint in her eyes.

"Never underestimate my goalie reflexes," I say, even though I'm a defenseman. But hey, who's counting?

The wind continues its rampage, toppling over a paint can this time. We both lunge for it, hands colliding as we steady the can together. Our fingers brush, and there's that spark again, that jolt of electricity I felt earlier.

"Good save," she quips, eyes locked on mine for a heartbeat longer than necessary.

"Teamwork," I reply, trying to ignore how the contact lingers, like the echo of a perfectly landed shot.

"Teamwork," she echoes, finally letting go.

The weather might be against us, but something tells me Lily Morgan and I can handle a lot more than a few mischievous gusts of wind. And as we all secure the equipment and battening down our little ship, I find myself looking forward to whatever challenge comes next. The way she rallies everyone together, it's like she's not just building a community garden, but a team—a community. And isn't that what hockey's all about? I find myself admiring her, not just for her looks—which are a bonus—but for her heart.

The sky darkens further, clouds rolling in with a menace that promises more than just a light sprinkle. Sure enough, within minutes, a downpour soaks through my sweatshirt, turning it a shade darker. I glance over at Lily, expecting to see irritation or frustration, but there's none. She simply laughs, shaking her head as if to dare the weather to do its worst.

"Alright, folks!" she calls out, her voice somehow rising above the roar of the rain. "Let's show this storm that it takes more than water to dampen our spirits! Grab those tarps! We'll cover the flower beds and tie them down. We won't let a bit of rain stop us."

I spring into action, securing the edges of a tarp alongside her, as do the others. Our hands work in tandem, tying knots with precision. We cover each bed, protecting the seedlings from the sudden, hard deluge.

"Nice knot," I comment, genuinely impressed by her swift handiwork.

"Thanks, I was a Girl Scout. Knots, campfires, and selling cookies—though I was always better at eating them," she quips, brushing wet strands of hair from her face.

"Good to know I have a survival expert on my team," I say, grateful for her quick thinking.

"Team?" she repeats, the word carrying weight in the sound of the relentless rain. "That's what we are today, aren't we?"

"Today and any other day you need me," I answer without hesitation, surprised at my own readiness to be part of her team, whatever form that might take.

We finish up with the tarps and step back to survey our handiwork. Despite the rain that has turned the day into an exercise in adaptability, the sense of achievement is tangible. For a moment, we stand side by side, watching the rain cascade off the protective plastic, safeguarding the fruits of our labor. Something shifts inside me, a realization that this woman who can ignite such cooperation in others has sparked something in me too. And I wonder what else we could accomplish together—if only the game of love were as straightforward as a game of hockey.

I take a sudden, impulsive chance.

“Hey, you want to grab a coffee? There’s a place just around the corner,” I suggest, peeling off my wet work gloves and tucking them into my back pocket.

Lily looks up, brushing a strand of chestnut hair from her face that had escaped her ponytail and is now stuck to her cheek. “I’d love to. I skipped lunch, and I could use something to warm me up."

We sprint, side by side but not quite touching, to a local coffee shop, a quaint little spot with steamed-up windows and the comforting aroma of roasted beans wafting through the door as we open it. The bell above chimes a welcome that seems to match Lily's bright energy—it's infectious, and I find myself smiling for no particular reason.

"Two large coffees, please," I say to the barista, and turn to Lily. "What do you take in yours?"

"Black, like my hockey soul," she jokes, and I laugh, surprised at the warmth that bubbles inside me at her quick wit.

"Make them both black then," I tell the barista. “Food?” I ask Lily.

She chooses soup and a club sandwich, and my stomach growls. I get the same, but add a bear claw.

As we wait, we sidle up to the pick-up counter, close enough that I can feel the warmth radiating from her despite the chill that still clings to my bones. The coffees come up quickly, and our hands reach for the same cardboard sleeve, fingers brushing in a fleeting caress that sends an unexpected jolt through me. She pulls away quickly, a blush creeping over her cheeks that has nothing to do with the cold.

"Sorry," she murmurs, and I shake my head.

"Don't be. It's... fine," I say, though 'fine' is hardly adequate to describe the current of electricity that just passed between us.

We take our coffees and claim a table by the window, watching as the world outside is painted in shades of gray by the relentless drizzle. It's cozy here, intimate, and as we sip our coffees, the conversation turns personal.

"Did you grow up playing hockey too?" I ask, remembering the way her eyes lit up talking about past community projects.

"Since I could walk," she replies with a chuckle. "Growing up here, in a town with more rinks than schools, it was inevitable. My dad was a pretty good player before his injury. He kind of lived vicariously through my slapshots after that."

"Sounds familiar," I say, nodding. "My folks were always supportive, pushing me to give back, you know? Hockey's been good to me, to us, but they made sure I knew there was more to life than what happens on the ice."

"Seems they did a good job," Lily says, her gaze steady on mine. It's unnerving and reassuring all at once, and I find myself lost in the depth of those eyes.

"Thanks," I mumble, feeling oddly vulnerable. "They tried their best."

We talk more about our families, sharing stories that draw laughter and sympathetic winces. It's easy, easier than I expected, and Lily's enthusiasm is a force of nature. I'm drawn to it, to her, like opposing poles of a magnet.

“And so now, here I am. Trying to move mountains—or, maybe I should say glaciers.”

"Your energy, it’s… it makes people want to be better. To do more," I confess, admiring how she's stirred the volunteers today, how she stirs something in me now. Right now, what's driving me is this inexplicable urge to keep seeing her smile, to hear her laugh. To be near her.

We finish our coffee. The sun is dipping low, and the rain has retreated. We take our time walking back to the park. The garden isn’t done, but there will be other days—and we’ve accomplished a lot today. Lily stands beside me one we arrive, her hair reflecting the dying light, a satisfied smile curving her lips.

"Look at that," she says, gesturing toward the playground where a group of kids are already clambering over the equipment we fixed up. "Instant payoff."

"Feels good," I admit, watching the community come alive around us. The ache in my muscles is evidence of the hard work, but it's the kind of ache that you welcome, the sort that speaks of effort and achievement.

"Thanks for being here today, Ethan," Lily turns to me, her green eyes earnest. "Your presence really represented the team well."

"Couldn't let you have all the fun," I quip, though in truth, I wouldn't have missed this for the world. Especially not when it meant spending time with her.

We linger a moment longer, basking in the success of the day. Kids laugh, volunteers pack up, and everything feels right in a way I hadn't expected when I first laced up my work boots this morning.

"Guess we should say our goodbyes, huh?" Lily breaks the comfortable silence between us. She bumps me with her hip, a gentle reminder of our proximity.

"Guess so." I stuff my hands into my jacket pockets, suddenly reluctant to end the day. There's an unexpected twinge in my chest, a sense of loss I can't quite place.

"See you at the rink tomorrow?" she asks, tilting her head slightly.

"Wouldn't miss it." Our eyes lock, and there's that subtle tension again, the one that's been building all day, ebbing and flowing like the tide.

"Good," she replies softly, then steps forward, bridging the gap between professionalism and something more personal as she wraps me in a hug. It's brief, but it's enough to send a jolt of warmth through me that has nothing to do with the coffee from earlier.

"Take care, Ethan," she says, pulling away but leaving a lingering touch on my arm.

"You too, Lily." I watch her walk away, her figure growing smaller. There's a feeling inside me that I can't shake off, a realization that I want these days to stretch on, that I want more than just the satisfaction of a job well done—I want the laughter, the banter, the shared looks over steaming cups of coffee.

I stride toward my truck, the chill of the evening creeping under my jacket and raising goosebumps on my skin. I can't shake off the image of Lily standing there among the volunteers, her hair windswept, smile wide. She's good at this—more than good—and it's impossible not to admire her for the way she brings everyone together.

But as the engine roars to life beneath me, my thoughts drift to Marco "Wild Shot" Silvestri, and that's where they snag. He had a meeting with her yesterday, and she avoided talking about it. I've seen him work his charm, and with someone like Lily... The grip on my steering wheel tightens, the leather groaning under the pressure. She'll be dealing with him closely, trying to smooth out the latest blunder he's danced himself into. The guy's got talent on the ice, but off it? He's a hurricane, leaving a trail of chaos. Is she ready for that? I wonder if maybe she's biting off more than she can chew with Marco. Guy’s a loose cannon, and Lily, well, she's sharp but not invincible. No one is.

The drive home is a blur of streetlights coming on and lengthening shadows, my mind replaying every moment spent with Lily today. The laughter, the easy conversation—it all felt right. Too right. And now, here I am, concerned about her tangled up with Marco's mess. But why? Is it because I'm worried about the team's reputation, or is it something else?

Maybe it's the way my stomach tightens when I picture them together. Maybe it's the way my hands want to clench into fists. Professional concern—that's what I should call it. But the honesty in the night air whispers another word to me: jealousy. It's a bitter taste in my mouth, unwanted and unexpected.

"Get a grip, Scott," I mutter to myself, shaking my head as if I could dislodge the thought. I don't have any claim over Lily. I barely know her. And yet, the idea of her laughing at something Marco said, or being charmed by that infamous smirk of his, it irks me more than it should.

The rearview mirror catches my eye, and for a moment, I meet my own gaze. There's a hard edge to it that I don't recognize, a protectiveness that goes beyond just teammates. Lily's capable, intelligent, and if anyone can handle Marco, it's her. So why does it feel like I want to be the one to make sure she doesn't get hurt?

I need to channel this energy into something productive, like the next match. Still, as I pull into my driveway and kill the engine, the silence that follows is heavy with unanswered questions. Tomorrow, I'll see Lily again, and maybe then I'll get a clearer picture.

For now, I let the darkness of the night envelop me, the stars above indifferent witnesses to the turmoil within.

CHAPTER SIX: MARCO

The party scene in the city is probably raging without me, but here I am, lounging on my leather couch like an old man, thanks to Lily's decree. The only company I've got tonight is my phone, and I'm not exactly thrilled about it. Scrolling through my feed, I'm looking for something—anything—to keep the boredom at bay. Then, there they are. Pictures of Lily and me, plastered all over social media, our smiles as staged as a sitcom laugh track.

"Wow," I murmur to the silent room, eyebrows lifting. We're a hit, or a miss, depending on who's looking. William managed to get some decent shots, even if I can still see the awkwardness. But maybe they're…passable?

It's bizarre seeing us like that, frozen in a moment that never really happened. The lighting is perfect, our bodies angled just so. If I didn't know any better, I'd buy into the fairytale too. But reality is a slapshot to the face, and this... well, this is just good marketing.

I dive into the comments, curiosity getting the best of me. "Let's see what the fans think," I mutter to myself, tapping on the screen.

"OMG, they look so cute together!" one comment reads, followed by a string of heart emojis. That's nice, I guess. A smile tugs at my lips. Lily would love that one—she's all about spreading that community cheer.

"Is this real? The Sabre's bad boy settling down?" another fan speculates. Settling down? I snort at the thought. If only they knew.

But then, the tide turns. "No chemistry," someone declares, their virtual voice dripping with disdain. "She looks more excited about the free food than him." Ouch. That one stings, even if it's half-true.

"Who wants to bet this is just a PR stunt?" another cynic chimes in. Bingo. But hey, you have to admit it's working. My feed hasn't been this lively since I scored that game-winner last season.

"Marco 'Wild Shot' Silvestri off the ice and playing it safe? Yeah, right!" That one actually makes me chuckle. They know me too well. Or do they?

"Looks forced," someone else comments. "And he is way out of her league, anyway." And suddenly, I'm defensive—not just for me, but for

Lily too. It was her idea, sure, but she's just doing her job. Besides, we might not be a couple, but Lily's passion for this game, for the team—it's as genuine as it gets. And I would consider us in the same league. I mean, I would date her. She might actually be *too good* for the likes of me.

"Give them a chance!" a hopeful sentiment pops up amidst the negativity. I appreciate the support, but it's hard to tell how much of this banter is fueled by actual interest in us or the thrill of potential drama.

"She could be the one," reads one of the comments, the words blurring as I rub my eyes, tired from the day's practice and this unexpected nighttime entertainment. Could she? Nah. It's all part of the game—the one off the ice.

"Keep dreaming," I whisper back to the silent question, locking my phone and tossing it onto the coffee table. It skids across the glass surface, coming to rest next to a stack of hockey magazines.

I stretch out and sink deeper into the couch. But as the quiet of the night wraps around me, I can't shake the feeling that these photos, these reactions—they're just the pregame show. The real action is yet to come.

I lay there for a moment before I pick my phone back up. If it gets the fans talking, then why not play along?

I tap out replies with practiced ease, the mischievous forward on the ice now playing defense in the digital world. "Thanks! Stay tuned for more," I type, adding a winking emoji for good measure. Can't let them down now; they're eating this up.

It's not just about deflecting slap shots anymore. I've got to maintain this image, keep the puck rolling. So, I pull up a photo from our last team huddle, the one where we're all leaning in, faces set with determination. Perfect.

"Your support means everything, folks," I post, along with the photo. "We're not just a team; we're a family. And we're going to fight for every win, on the ice and off. Sabres together." Send.

It's a different kind of playbook, but the strategy is clear: bring the fans into our locker room, let them feel the camaraderie. With a sigh, I lean back, running a hand through my hair. This whole marketing ploy with Lily—it's clever, sure. But there's a part of me that wants to text her now, to peel back the curtain and see what she's really thinking behind those green eyes.

"Too soon, Wild Shot," I mutter. *Play it cool, Marco. Don't get caught up in your own head games.* Instead, I draft a message to our social media manager.

Got some ideas to rally the fans. Let's chat in the morning about next steps. We've got momentum; let's use it.

Sent. That should do it. Keep the conversation going, keep the ice alive even when the arena's dark. Tomorrow, we skate; tonight, we strategize. It's all part of the game—the one that's playing out in the rink of public opinion.

And as for Lily? Well, the game's just getting started.

***

The ice is a different world at dawn, the rink a canvas of untouched potential. My blades carve fresh lines into the surface as I glide across it, the chill biting through my jersey and waking up every sense in my body. This is where I belong, where all the noise fades and it's just me, the puck, and the promise of that next shot.

"Silvestri! Focus!" Coach bellows from the sidelines, snapping me back to reality.

I swerve, puck on my stick, and let loose a slapshot that rings off the post with a satisfying clang. The boys hoot their approval, and the sound echoes under the high ceilings of the arena. Practice has been intense this morning, everyone skating double time, knowing that eyes are on us now more than ever, thanks to the Lily Morgan effect.

"Hey, Wild Shot," Alex, one of our wingers, calls out as we take a breather by the boards, "Heard you're playing Romeo off the ice."

"Give it up, Ace," I shoot back with a grin, shrugging off his jab. "You know the tabloids are just fishing for a love story where there isn't one."

"Come on, man," another chimes in, "those pictures looked pretty cozy to me!"

"Staged romance is just part of the game plan," I retort, but the smirk on my face doesn't quite reach my eyes. It's not entirely true, and somewhere inside, the notion stirs an unfamiliar mix of thrill and apprehension.

"Is it staged, though?" Ethan's voice cuts through the banter, serious enough to draw our attention. His bright blue eyes are earnest, concerned. "Those comments online, they can get nasty. We don't need that kind of distraction, especially now. Is this something you and Lily planned?"

"Look," I start, leaning against the cool plexiglass, "I know some folks aren't buying what we're selling. But this buzz—it's good for us. Gets people talking, gets them invested." I avoid answering about Lily's plans. And I don't quite like Ethan's tone, but I shake it off. I tap my chest right over the team logo. "We've got to use this momentum, turn it into something positive. Who cares about a few trolls when we have a city of fans behind us?"

"You've got a point," Ethan concedes, nodding slowly. "But we gotta keep our heads in the game."

"Exactly," I affirm, pushing off the boards and back onto the ice, feeling the weight of leadership settle onto my shoulders like a mantle. "Let's show 'em what we're made of. Use the hype, fuel the fire, and bring the heat where it matters—right here on the ice."

There's a collective murmur of agreement, and the energy shifts, refocused. We fall back into drills, passing and shooting with a renewed vigor. Each snap of the puck is a statement, each save a battle cry.

As practice winds down and we leave the rink, sweat-soaked and exhausted, I think about Lily. There's a game being played alright, one with higher stakes than any scoreboard could capture. And whether I like it or not, Lily and I are teammates now—navigating not just the slippery ice, but also the even more treacherous ground of public opinion.

"Hit the showers, boys," coach yells. "Press is out there. Time to smile pretty."

***

The flashbulbs pop like a string of firecrackers as I step up to the podium, the glare almost as blinding as the ice during an afternoon game. The sea of reporters before me is a frenzy of movement and noise, each one clamoring for the scoop. There are a dozen microphones in front of me.

"Marco," one reporter shouts above the rest, "what can you tell us about the photos with Lily Morgan?"

I lean into the cluster of microphones, my voice steady despite the heat of the lights. "Lily's been a fantastic addition to our team's dynamic off the rink," I say, choosing my words carefully. "She brings passion and innovation to our marketing strategies, and honestly, we're lucky to have her."

"Are those pictures part of the strategy?" another reporter probes, her pen poised like she's ready to skewer me with it.

"Well," I reply with a grin that's all charm, no surrender. "It's all about engaging with the community, getting the fans excited about our games. We need their support now more than ever. And if fans like seeing us together? Come to the games. She's there for every one now. I won't comment on our personal attachment."

"Has this affected the team's focus?"

"Not in the least." I stand tall, shoulders back, embodying the confidence I want to project. "We're dedicated to improving our performance on the ice. That's where our true focus lies."

As I field more questions, deflecting and bantering with practiced ease, my thoughts drift to Lily. Her green eyes that miss nothing, her chestnut hair that seems to catch fire in the sunlight. How she matches my wit and challenges me without missing a beat.

When the press conference wraps up, I make my way through the bowels of the arena to the team's office. Lily's already there, perched on the edge of a desk, her keen gaze poring over a stack of papers. The room hums with the tension of unspoken words.

"Hey," I greet, leaning against the doorframe.

"Hi, Marco," she says, looking up. There's a spark in her eyes that tells me she's ready to get down to business. "Ready to brainstorm?"

"Lead the way, coach," I quip, but I'm not entirely joking. She has this pull, an undeniable gravity, and whether it's strategizing or skating, I find myself wanting to follow her lead.

We dive into the discussion, tossing around ideas for fan events, charity matches, social media takeovers. Our heads are bent close together, the energy between us crackling like static before a lightning strike. She notably doesn't comment on the pictures—or what I said during the presser.

"Maybe we could do a series of meet-and-greets," she suggests. "Show the fans that their support means everything to us."

"Sounds good," I agree. "And what if you were there? What if we ramped up the drama? A few more 'candid' shots of us out together?"

The word 'together' hangs in the air, thick with implication. Our eyes lock, and for a fleeting second, the room fades away. It's just Lily and me, and the sudden awareness of how right it feels to be this close.

“I mean, I’m assuming you saw the reaction to our photos? Someone even asked if you were *the one*…”

“Marco…” Her eyes go wide.

I think, impulsively, of kissing her. Then the spell breaks, her phone chirping with a reminder, and we both pull back, returning to the safety of professionalism.

"Right," she says, clearing her throat. "The photos worked, but let's keep the focus on hockey, though. We don't want to distract from the game."

"Of course," I respond as she stands to answer her phone. Maybe, just maybe, the real distraction is sitting right in front of me.

CHAPTER SEVEN: LILY

The fluorescent lights of the office buzz overhead. It's not even seven in the morning, and I'm already pumped with the kind of energy that can only come from a double shot of espresso and an optimistic belief in the day ahead. The hockey season is heating up, and so are my strategies to pack the stands and ignite community spirit.

"Early bird gets the worm, or in this case, the puck," I mutter to myself, dropping my bag with a thud and firing up my computer.

But as I settle into my chair, something feels off. There's a shift in the air, a crackle that's out of place in the stillness of our usually dormant early morning office. I swivel around, scanning the space, and that's when I see it—Krista, one of the marketing assistants, with her icy blonde bob perfectly coiffed, leaning against Mr. Thompson's desk.

Their heads are close together, too close for a casual morning catch-up, and his laughter echoes across the room, bouncing off walls lined with framed jerseys and action shots of our hockey greats. A sour taste creeps into my mouth, and I tighten my grip on the armrests of my chair.

"Of course she's here," I whisper under my breath. Krista, ever the strategist, knows the power of first impressions and last-minute pitches. She's been standoffish—if not a little snobby—since I arrived. Whispers in the office are that she was up for my job before I cinched it.

Her piercing blue eyes flick to mine, catching me in the act of observing them. She fires off a smug smile my way, one that says she's already ten steps ahead.

"Stay calm, Lily," I coach myself, trying to shake off the unsettling sensation. I know better than to let Krista get under my skin. Years of playing hockey have taught me to keep my eye on the puck, not the players aiming for a body check.

I give my screen a purposeful glance, clicking through the presentation I've spent weeks perfecting. It's full of the distillation of all of my ideas for community event ideas, ones that showcase not just the strength of our players, but also the heart of the town that supports them. It's good—no, it's gold-medal-round-in-the-Olympics good. But

Krista's presence, her aura of confidence as she shares a private joke with Mr. Thompson, chips away at my certainty.

I force my attention back to the glow of the monitor, but the image of Krista, all ambition and hidden agendas, lingers at the edge of my vision like a rival player waiting to steal the puck. This office may not be an ice rink, but the competition is just as fierce, and I'm not about to let Krista—or anyone else—slide an unchecked goal past me.

Taking a deep breath, I rise from my desk with the kind of determination that's fueled many third-period comebacks on the rink. My fingers grip the edges of my meticulously organized folder, the pages inside brimming with potential. This isn't just about marketing.

"Mr. Thompson," I call out as I approach his open office door, my voice steady despite the thunder of nerves I feel hammering against my ribs.

"Ah, Lily! Come in, come in. What have you got for me today?" His voice is warm like a coach's before a big game, but his eyes flicker to the side briefly, catching Krista's smirk.

"Community engagement ideas," I reply, ignoring the chill from Krista's corner of the room. "The community garden project was great, so I was thinking we could set up a series of hockey clinics—"

"Free for kids, right?" he interjects, leaning back in his chair, fingers tented in front of him.

"Exactly," I nod eagerly, encouraged by his quick uptake. "Led by our players. It'll be great PR, especially with Marco's growing fanbase, and there's nothing like giving back to build team spirit."

"Uh-huh." Mr. Thompson nods, but his gaze drifts over my shoulder, where I can only imagine Krista stands, oozing confidence like she owns the place—and maybe even him.

"Also, an idea for a charity match," I continue, trying to reel him back in. "We partner with local businesses, raise funds for the community center—they're struggling to keep their after-school programs running."

"Charity match," he repeats, though it sounds more like he's rehearsing the words rather than considering them.

"Think about it, sir," I press on, feeling the ground beneath me grow shaky. "It's a win-win. Good for the town, good for the team's image."

"Right, right." Mr. Thompson's response carries the weight of a deflected puck, hollow and off-target.

"Is everything okay?" I chance the question, my eyes locking onto his in search of the usual spark, the one that says he's with me on this, that he sees the vision. But all I find is a weariness, as if he's tired of this game we're playing, one I didn't even realize had started.

"Of course, Lily," he assures me with a tight smile that doesn't quite reach his eyes. My stomach knots tighter.

"Great, so—" I try to circle back to my pitch, but Krista's shadow looms larger now, her presence an unspoken barrier between my enthusiasm and Mr. Thompson's attention. She's not even in his office—but somehow, she is. I don't know what's going on.

"Let's touch base later, Lily. Got a lot to chew on here," he says, standing up—a clear signal that my time is up.

"Sure thing, Mr. Thompson." My words are automatic, the disappointment a sharp sting I refuse to show. I turn to leave, the smugness in Krista's silent victory lap slicing through me. But I don't let it slow my stride. No, the day is far from over, and I'm not one to forfeit after the first period. Let the games begin, Krista. I'm just getting warmed up.

I stride across the plush carpet of the office, each step measured and deliberate. Krista's desk looms ahead, a sleek expanse of glass and chrome in the middle of the main admin bullpen that seems to mirror her icy demeanor. She's perched on the edge of her swivel chair, like a queen overlooking her court, all sharp angles and polished surfaces.

"Krista," I begin, my voice steady despite the drumbeat of my heart against my ribs. "We need to talk."

She doesn't look up from the screen immediately, continuing to tap away at her keyboard with a manicured precision. When she does deign to glance at me, it's with an air of feigned surprise that doesn't quite reach her piercing blue eyes.

"Talk? About what, Lily?" she asks, her tone light, almost airy. It grates against my nerves, but I push through.

"About what's going on here with Mr. Thompson," I say, folding my arms across my chest. "I feel like you're trying to undermine my community event proposals."

Krista leans back, her posture relaxed as she gives a dismissive wave of her hand. "Undermine? You give me too much credit," she says, a smirk playing on her lips.

She sidesteps direct confrontation with the grace of a seasoned politician. But I'm not in the mood for dancing.

"Cut the act," I press on. "I saw the way he brushed off my ideas. Ideas, I might add, that have always been met with enthusiasm before."

"Maybe they're just not that good this time," Krista shrugs, feigning concern. "You know how it is, the same old play gets predictable after a while."

Her words are a check into the boards, meant to rattle me, but I hold my ground. She lets out a soft, calculated sigh, tapping a finger against her chin as if considering something profound.

"Of course, I've been working on some new angles myself," she muses aloud. "Fresh strategies. It's essential to keep things... invigorating, don't you think?"

The implication hangs between us, unsaid yet crystal clear. She's hinting that her ideas are superior, that she'll be the one breathing new life into our campaigns. I can almost see the threads of doubt she's trying to weave around me, about me, but I refuse to let them take hold.

"Sure, innovation is key," I agree, locking onto her gaze with a challenge. "But so is integrity and teamwork. I guess we'll see which approach wins out in the end."

"Struggling to keep up with the real talent?" Krista's voice slices through my focus, smooth and sharp as a skate blade.

My eyes narrow just slightly. "Actually, I was just reflecting on how teamwork often trips up solo skaters," I shoot back, the corner of my mouth twitching upward. "You know, since they're too busy checking their own reflection in the ice."

Her laugh is airy, dismissive, but I catch the slight falter in it. Score one for team spirit. Her smile never wavers, but there's a flash of something—irritation, perhaps—in those icy depths. For a moment, we're just two rivals acknowledging the game, the unspoken understanding that neither of us will back down.

Her voice is silk over steel. "May the best strategy prevail."

With that, I pivot on my heel and walk away. I stride back to my office, the cool air of the office calming the heat flaring in my chest. Krista's veiled jabs have left me simmering, but I've played on colder rinks than this and come out on top. The chatter around me fades into white noise as I pull up the community event proposal on my screen, my fingers poised above the keys.

The morning drags on, punctuated by the tapping of keyboards and the occasional hushed discussion. I can feel the shift in the room, an electric undercurrent that wasn't there before. It's as if Krista's perfume has somehow become part of the office's central air, sweetly suffocating. As I pass by the water cooler, snippets of conversation reach my ears—a mention of Krista's name here, whispers about me and Marco there.

I press on, determined not to let the whispers cloud my judgment. At the end of the day, it's not about whose voice is loudest, but whose ideas can score when it matters most. And like any good player, I'm all about the endgame.

I'm ensconced once again in spreadsheets and permits for more city project proposals when my phone buzzes. Mr. Thompson's name flashes on the screen, sending a jolt straight to my gut.

"Mr. Thompson," I answer, my fingers tightening around the receiver.

"Lily, please come to my office. There's something we need to address," his voice is as smooth as freshly Zambonied ice, but there's an edge to it that makes me wary.

"Of course, I'll be right there."

As I enter his office, Mr. Thompson doesn't waste time on pleasantries. "Lily, this tension between you and Krista—it needs to end. We're all on the same team here."

His words skate close to accusation, and I can almost hear the slapshot of Krista's influence finding the back of the net. But I refuse to let it rattle me.

"Mr. Thompson, I'm here to do my job and to do it well. Any rivalry isn't part of my game plan," I reply, standing my ground even as my mind races.

"Good. Keep it professional. I don't want to hear any more that this is creating an uncomfortable work environment."

That little rat...I think.

"Now, what's next for Marco? We've got folks turning a little, but his image could use some more polishing, given his... colorful reputation," he leans back, steepling his fingers as he watches me closely.

"Marco's got heart, and the fans love him. They just need to see the man behind the myth," I say, feeling the familiar surge of excitement at the challenge. "We're working on boosting his community presence—showing his dedication, both on and off the ice."

"Excellent," Mr. Thompson nods, but his gaze is calculating. "Keep up the good work, Lily. And remember… no more office rivalry."

"Understood," I say, even as my mind flickers over the statistics, the strategies, the narratives we could weave for Marco. The game is on, and I'm not just here to play—I'm here to win. I stop in the doorway.

"Actually, there's an outing tomorrow," I begin, leaning forward over the plush chair across from Mr. Thompson's grand, mahogany desk. The air in his office is heavy, laced with the scent of leather and old books. "It's a charity event, but with a twist. Marco will be on a fake date."

"A fake date?" Mr. Thompson raises an eyebrow, his curiosity piqued.

"Yep." I nod, tapping a finger against my knee as I pitch the idea. "We're aiming to show his softer side, appeal to the fans. It's staged, but the chemistry has to look real. It'll be plastered all over social media, get people talking for all the right reasons."

"Interesting tactic." He leans back in his chair, the creak of leather punctuating the silence. "I suppose if it humanizes him, turns down the heat on some of his more recent... antics, it could work."

"Exactly." I'm determined to keep my voice steady, to sound as confident as I need to be. I can't afford a crack in my armor, not when Krista's shadow looms like a pending storm cloud over every move I make. I refuse to let Krista—or anyone, for that matter—undermine my efforts or the team's potential. I'm here for the long haul, for the wins we're going to net both on the ice and in the hearts of our community.

"Good. That'll be all then," Mr. Thompson dismisses me with a wave, already reaching for a stack of papers on his desk.

As I push off the chair and stride out the door, the game plan for tomorrow's event rolls through my mind—or rather, the lack of a plan. I need to find a charity event, *fast*. And I need to tell Marco to polish up his dress shoes.

And as for Krista, she's about to find out that I'm much more than just an adversary in the office—I'm the playmaker who's about to score the winning goal.

CHAPTER EIGHT: LILY

I adjust the strap of my purse and take a deep breath, steadying myself as I approach the entrance to the rink. This is it—the first fake date with Marco "Wild Shot" Silvestri. It's all staged for the cameras, but my stomach flutters with real nerves. How are we going to pull this off? Will our back-and-forth be convincing enough? The chill from the ice seeps through the walls, familiar and oddly comforting, and I remind myself that I'm in my element here—hockey is my blood.

I'm meeting him outside the locker room, and we're going straight to the gala, being held to benefit a local hospital. *Incredibly* luckily, the tickets were another win from my magazine friend.

The door swings open, and there he is. Marco leans against the wall, his dark hair tousled perfectly, those deep brown eyes glinting with a hint of mischief. He stands out like a celebrity at a hometown game—confident, bright in the fluorescent lighting of the rink foyer. And then there's his attire, a tuxedo that fits him impeccably, molding to his form in a way that suggests both elegance and an easy, athletic grace. It's not what I expected, but Marco wears it as naturally as if it were his second skin, adding an air of sophistication to his rugged charm.

His smile spreads slowly as he catches sight of me, disarming and warm. It's a smile that could melt the ice. I'm glad that I dressed up, too, the silk dress that I hadn't found much use for since a friend's wedding last summer now seeming the perfect pick.

The tuxedo makes a striking statement; it's sharply tailored, enhancing his broad shoulders and lean physique. The contrast of his casual, mischievous demeanor with the formal, precise cut of the fabric is jarring yet oddly fitting. It's as if he's walked off a movie set, the dashing lead who's about to sweep the heroine off her feet, except this is no movie, and I'm no damsel. Yet, the sight of him in that very nicely fitted tuxedo sends an unexpected flutter through me, and a touch of admiration for his bold fashion choice tonight.

"Hey, Lily," he greets, voice smooth as a fresh Zamboni sweep. "You look beautiful. Ready to play the part?"

His charm wraps around me like a cozy scarf on a brisk winter day, easing the tightness in my chest. I let out the breath I didn't realize I was holding and feel my lips twitch into a smile.

"Only if you can keep up with my acting skills," I quip, feeling my nerves settle. Humor—that's how I'll navigate through this.

Marco pushes off the wall, closing the distance between us with a few easy strides. I notice the way he moves—graceful despite his size, a testament to years on the ice—and I'm momentarily taken aback by the thoughtfulness in his gaze. It's a look that speaks of depth beyond the tabloid tales, and it piques my curiosity about who Marco Silvestri really is, beneath the swagger.

"Trust me, Lily," he says, his voice tinged with a playful confidence that's infectious, "keeping up has never been my problem."

And just like that, he sets the tone for the evening: light, teasing, and unexpectedly reassuring. I find myself looking forward to what comes next, eager to peel back the layers of Marco's carefully crafted public image. Maybe, just maybe, this won't be as daunting as I thought.

We take my car to the restaurant that's hosting the gala, and heads turn when we arrive together.

"Everyone's staring, darling," I say, testing the waters of our pretend rapport. "I hope it's for a good reason and not because you've been up to mischief."

Marco winks, a gleam of mischief dancing in his deep brown eyes. "Mischief? Do you know what that is? You think spreadsheets are as exciting as a faceoff."

I laugh, the sound mingling with the ambient noise of the restaurant we're seated at. This is all for show, a staged date to boost Marco's image and, admittedly, give my community projects the spotlight they need. But the way Marco tosses jokes around like hockey pucks across the ice feels far too genuine for comfort. Or maybe that's just his skill at play.

"Spreadsheets can be thrilling," I counter, my voice laced with exaggerated fervor. "The thrill of organization, the adrenaline rush of a well-crafted graph..."

"Adrenaline rush?" Marco feigns shock, clutching his chest. "You need to get out more."

"Hey, I get out plenty," I say, though I'm starting to realize how much of my life has revolved around hockey teams and not enough around... well, living. In fact, since my dad passed, I know I've withdrawn. But anyone would—right?

"Sure you do," he says, a teasing edge to his tone. "And I bet you think a power play is when you plug in your laptop before it dies, right?"

"Ha-ha," I drawl. "Very funny, Wild Shot."

"Please, Lily, call me Marco," he insists, leaning in closer. "We're on a date after all, even if it's only make-believe."

As I meet his gaze, something flutters in my stomach—a rogue butterfly that doesn't understand this is just an act. I push the feeling aside, focusing on the playful banter that seems to flow effortlessly between us now.

"Okay, *Marco*," I acquiesce with a mock-serious nod. "But only because 'Wild Shot' sounds like a bad cowboy movie."

He throws his head back and laughs—a rich, warm sound that fills the space between us and smooths over any lingering awkwardness. His laughter is contagious, and I find myself joining in, the sound of our combined mirth drawing the attention of the restaurant patrons.

"Looks like we've really got ourselves an audience," Marco murmurs, his smile broadening as he nods toward a table by the window. A couple of locals have their phones out, snapping pictures in our direction. The flash is subtle, but it's there, a reminder that this date is as much for them as it is for us.

"Let's give them a good show then," I say, raising my glass in a toast. "To successful staging and the fine line between fiction and reality."

"Cheers to that," Marco agrees, tapping his glass against mine. The clink echoes like a puck hitting the boards, solid and sure.

For a moment, as we sit sipping our drinks and slipping into comfortable conversation, I forget we're performing. Marco's charm is disarming, and his humor is a refreshing break from the serious, often solitary world of team turnarounds. It's a game we're playing, but for the first time since stepping into this rink of deception, I feel like I might actually enjoy myself.

The clattering of dishes and the low hum of conversation fade into the background as Marco leans forward, resting his elbows on the table. The dim lights of the dining room cast a soft glow over his olive skin, highlighting the earnestness in his deep brown eyes.

"Seriously though, Lily, that idea you have about the youth hockey clinics in underprivileged areas – it's brilliant. It's exactly what this community needs," he says, and I detect no hint of the playboy persona he often projects. Instead, I'm met with sincerity, a side of Marco that's as surprising as it is intriguing.

"I really believe hockey can be more than just a game for kids. It can teach them life skills, give them a sense of belonging," I respond, feeling a swell of pride for my work. I've always seen sports as a catalyst for positive change, and hearing Marco echo that sentiment sends an unexpected sense of camaraderie through me.

"Belonging... Yeah, I get that." He nods slowly, his voice tinged with something that sounds like nostalgia. "I wouldn't be where I am today without those rink rats I grew up with in Chicago. They were my family, in a way."

His words tug at something inside me. I think of Ethan then, his commitment to giving back, his bright blue eyes always looking out for his teammates, on and off the ice. Ethan suggesting events at the diner, without having to be dragged kicking and screaming like bad-boy Marco. Both men, so different and yet so alike in their passion for the game.

"Marco, I—" I start, but the words catch in my throat, the ambivalence gnawing at me. Here sits Marco, revealing layers I hadn't expected, while thoughts of Ethan circle in my mind. Can I truly be considering both men? Or is the allure of the unexpected drawing me in? "There's some turmoil in the offices, so I'm not sure how many of my ideas might make it to fruition right now…"

"Hey, it's okay," Marco interjects. "We'll make it happen. Together."

"Right. Together," I echo, my voice steadier than I feel. Because despite the confusion, maybe, just maybe, I'm starting to see Marco not just as the 'Wild Shot' on the ice, but as a partner in this crazy endeavor.

Our dinner is served in courses, and every one is excellent. Marco has exquisite manners, and is a good conversationalist. If I weren't aware that this was fake, I might have been tricked into thinking this was a *real* date. But it does end, and reality waits.

It's been an evening filled with surprises, not least of which is how much I actually enjoy Marco's company when he's not living up to his 'Wild Shot' moniker.

"Thanks for tonight," I say, sliding out of the fancy chair with a grace I don't feel. "You were... surprisingly charming."

Marco rises too, his smile easy and genuine. "Only 'surprisingly'?" He arches an eyebrow, that mischievous glint in his deep brown eyes making my heart do a weird little flip.

"You've been known to turn on the charm when it suits you." I roll my eyes, but I can't wipe the smirk off my face.

"True," he concedes, shrugging his shoulders in a way that tells me he's not really sorry. "But hey, before we call it a night, what do you say we grab some dessert? There's this bakery just around the corner, makes the best cannoli you'll ever taste." His suggestion is casual, but there's an undercurrent of eagerness that's hard to miss.

I hesitate, biting my lip. This wasn't part of the plan. The gala, be seen—that was it. But the idea of spending more time with him—off the clock, so to speak—sparks a thrill in my chest I can't ignore. "Are you asking me out on a real date, Marco Silvestri?"

He chuckles, holding his hands up as if to ward off the implication. "No, no, just as friends." He pauses, watching me closely. "Unless you're afraid to be seen with me without a contract involved?"

"Ha!" The sound bursts from me before I can stop it, and I shake my head. "Afraid? Please, I've faced down tougher opponents than you on the ice."

"Is that a yes then?" His eyes twinkle with challenge and something else—a warmth that seems too sincere to be faked.

"Fine," I acquiesce, feeling a rush of anticipation mixed with a twinge of nervousness. "But only because I'm curious about these world-class cannoli."

"Excellent." His grin stretches wider, and he holds out his arm. "Shall we?"

I link my arm through his, allowing myself this moment of spontaneity. "Lead the way."

As we step out into the cool night air, I'm acutely aware of the heat of Marco's body next to mine. We're walking closer than strictly necessary, our steps in sync as we head toward the promise of sweet treats and, possibly, something even sweeter—genuine friendship. Or maybe, just maybe, the beginnings of something more.

***

The door to "La Dolce Vita" chimes its welcome, pulling me into a world where powdered sugar dances in the air and the golden glow of hanging lights casts a warm hue on everything it touches. I inhale deeply, the scent of freshly baked pastries mingling with the bitter notes of espresso, and my senses come alive.

Marco leads the way to a small table tucked away in the corner, the kind that invites close conversation and shared secrets. We slide into our seats, a basket of cannoli taking center stage between us. The delicate shells, filled with sweetened ricotta, are dusted with pistachios and chocolate shavings—artful to the eye, promising indulgence.

"Okay, so these world-class cannoli you were bragging about?" I tease, picking one up and examining it like it's a piece of evidence. "They better live up to the hype."

"Trust me, they will," Marco says, his confidence as rich as the dessert in front of us.

We both take a bite, and for a moment, there's nothing but the crunch of pastry and the mmm of satisfaction. It tastes like victory, like something earned rather than given, and it's delicious.

"Alright, you win this round, Silvestri," I admit, smiling despite myself.

"Right," Marco nods, suddenly serious, his eyes locking onto mine with an intensity that makes my heart beat faster. "This community service project—it means a lot to you, doesn't it?"

"More than you know," I confess, feeling the weight of my own expectations. "It's about rebuilding connections, making people feel like they're part of something bigger. But office politics are tricky right now. Not something I expected to deal with."

"That's a shame. I've seen firsthand how sports can bring people together. Hockey isn't just a game; it's a lifeline for some kids. It teaches them discipline, teamwork, respect." His words echo my deepest beliefs, and I'm drawn to the fervor in his voice. Marco is more than a charming athlete; he's someone who knows the game's value beyond the ice.

"Have you considered starting a youth league? For those who don't have access to the expensive club teams?" I suggest, excitement bubbling within me.

"Thought about it? I've sketched out plans," he reveals, pulling his phone out and waking it to reveal a detailed diagram. "But I haven't found the right partner to make it happen."

"Until now," I say quietly, looking over the blueprint of dreams yet to be realized. "Let's make this a reality."

He smiles at that, a smile that's genuine and full of promise. "You have no idea how good it feels to hear you say that."

There's something about Marco—the way he speaks with conviction, challenges norms, and refuses to hide behind his public persona—that breaks through my professional facade. He's done this before, that much is clear. There's a history in the way he talks about his plans, a personal stake that he's not quite ready to share. He didn't say that he had these plans when we first met—and I wonder why.

But tonight isn't about prying open past wounds; it's about planning for a brighter future. And a league? Instead of just photo-ops? That could be big. The start of something that gains momentum, becomes a legacy.

The remnants of our desserts—now ignored—sit between us. Marco leans back in his chair, one arm slung over the back, his expression earnest as he speaks about the youth mentorship program he envisions. "You know, get them on the ice, teach them a few moves... but more than that, show them how to work together, be part of something positive."

I find myself nodding along, not just in agreement, but in admiration. The man who's been labeled a 'Wild Shot' for his antics on and off the ice is sitting across from me, discussing the importance of community and connection with such fervor that it's hard to reconcile this version of Marco with the tabloid tales.

"Sounds like you've given this a lot of thought," I say, not able to keep the surprise out of my voice.

"Does it?" He raises an eyebrow with a playful smirk, but there's a glint of something more—pride, maybe? "Lily, I want to make a difference, not just headlines. I know I don't always act like it."

It's then that I feel the shift, like a puck gliding smoothly from one end of the rink to the other. My reservations about Marco Silvestri are fading, melting away under the warmth of his genuine desire to do good. And darn it, if that doesn't make him more attractive. It's not just his olive skin or those deep brown eyes; it's the heart behind the mischief that's winning me over.

"Marco," I start, finding the courage to voice my thoughts, "you're full of surprises. In a good way."

"Only trying to keep up with you, Morgan." His grin is infectious, and I return it.

"Finish your dessert," he says. "I have it on good authority that if you're out too late, you turn into a spreadsheet about pumpkins."

I laugh, but oblige. After we're done, we stand up, gathering our coats as we prepare to leave the bakery. The air outside is brisk, a reminder of the winter season, but there's a warmth inside me that has little to do with the heated interior we're leaving behind.

"Tonight was..." I search for the right word, looking up at the sky where a few stars have dared to twinkle despite the city lights. "Inspiring."

"Agreed," Marco says, falling into step beside me. "You know, I'm actually looking forward to our next... collaboration."

I like the sound of it. "Yeah, me too. There's a lot we can do together, Marco."

"Definitely," he agrees, and I see the outline of his profile softened by the streetlights, the enthusiasm in his eyes unmistakable. "Listen, I want to walk a bit. I'll catch a taxi back. But let me walk you to your car."

I nod. As we reach the corner, Marco turns to me, his hands tucked into his pockets.

"So, until next time, Ms. Morgan?"

"Until next time, Mr. Silvestri," I reply, feeling a sense of rightness about this whole crazy arrangement. I know without a doubt that I genuinely enjoy Marco's company. His drive matches my own, his dedication inspires me, and the prospect of what we could achieve together sends a thrill through me. It's a hat trick of potential.

He holds the car door for me, and as the door closes next to me, the sound of the lock clicking into place echoes in the space—a definitive punctuation to an evening that's left my thoughts scattered. He smiles and waves, and I watch him walk away, loosening his tie. I start the car, gripping the steering wheel as if it can anchor me amid the swirling currents of my emotions.

I've always considered myself good at reading the ice—anticipating where the puck is going to be, knowing how the game will unfold. But now, when it comes to my heart, I'm not sure if I'm playing offense or defense.

Marco...It was supposed to be just for show, all part of the strategy to boost his image, nothing more than a clever play. But tonight, sitting across from him, watching his hands animate each word he spoke, I saw beyond the facade. His passion isn't just for the game on the ice—it's for the people around it. And it's infectious.

Yet there's Ethan, too—steady and true as the blue line. The way he champions causes without seeking the spotlight speaks volumes of his character. With Ethan, it's like we're in sync, a seamless pass that could lead to the perfect goal. The truth is, they both make me want to be better—to dig deeper, to reach further. Marco challenges me with his intensity, his unexpected depth beneath that mischievous grin. And Ethan steadies me with his support, his genuine kindness that never seems to falter.

The car is silent, save for the distant hum of the city nightlife outside, yet inside my head, it's a cacophony of what-ifs and maybes. This isn't a game I can win with a well-timed slapshot or a strategic check against the boards. This is life—messy, unpredictable, and frighteningly real.

My phone buzzes, and I flinch at the sudden intrusion. It's probably just a friend checking in or a reminder about tomorrow's schedule from my calendar. But part of me wonders if it's Marco... or Ethan. This isn't hockey; this is my heart. And right now, I'm not entirely sure what my game plan is.

CHAPTER NINE: ETHAN

A transfer offer?

The news, delivered pre-game by the coach, hits me like a slap shot to the chest, sharp and sudden. Whispers ricochet around the locker room as if the walls themselves are quivering with the impending change. My teammates huddle in small clusters, their murmurs an anxious soundtrack to the chaos that's unfolding. I see their concerned glances flick my way, but I can't quite bring myself to meet their eyes just yet.

"Hey, Ethan, what gives?" Lucas's question, barely louder than a breath, cuts through the tension. I ignore it as I dress for the game.

"Is it true?" Damon's voice chimes in, a mix of disbelief and worry lacing the words.

I rub a hand over my face, still in my gear, the weight of my pads suddenly feeling like a mountain upon my shoulders. The cold, familiar scent of sweat and equipment does nothing to comfort me this time.

My fists clench at my sides, the leather of my gloves groaning under the strain. I can hear my heart pounding against my chest protector—thud, thud, thud—as if it's trying to break free from the cage of ribs surrounding it.

This team... these guys... they're more than just a roster of players; they're my brothers on ice. Every check into the boards, every shared victory and loss, every moment we've spent fighting for that puck has bound us together. To think I might have to leave them behind—it's like considering leaving a part of myself in the rink, frozen beneath the ice.

I glance up, finally letting my gaze drift across the room. Their faces are a blur of helmets and jerseys, but each one is etched into my memory. This isn't how I imagined it might end. Not with rumors and whispered fears, but with a bang—a final horn sounding off our last game together, whenever that may be.

I stay silent. We all shuffle out to the bench, and the sound of the crowd—bigger now, thanks to Lily—ricochets in my head. It's my senior year, so a transfer is unusual. But a bigger school, a degree from a more prestigious name—the possibility of pro scouts. My mind is swirling.

"Scott, you okay?" The coach's voice breaks through my spiraling thoughts, grounding me back to the harsh reality of the situation.

"Yeah," I lie, forcing a tight smile that doesn't reach my bright blue eyes. "Just taking it all in."

Taking in the possibility of a transfer—of abandoning the very ice that has become my second home. The thought alone is enough to furrow my brow, creasing lines of stress across my forehead that feel like they're carved in ice.

But I have to stay strong for them, for the fans who chant my name, for the family that taught me to give back as much as I've been given. With a resolve that feels as brittle as the ice beneath my skates, I push off the bench, my movements deliberate and steady.

"Let's focus on the game," I say to my teammates, hoping to steady the ship in the midst of this brewing storm. "We've got a job to do." And with that, I lead by example, striding out onto the ice, where the world makes sense and the only transfers I want to think about are passes to my teammates.

The ice resounds with the echo of our discontent, whispers skittering like a puck across the slick surface. I catch bits and pieces of my teammates' conversations on the bench, their concern for me slicing through the cold air sharper than any skate.

"Man, what are we going to do without Ethan anchoring defense?"

Alex's voice breaks, the words heavy with the weight of uncertainty.

"Can't believe this is happening. Scott's the backbone of this team," Noah says, the sentiment rippling like a rogue wave.

I'm right here, traversing the rink, yet I feel miles away from these guys I've bled with on this very ice. Their voices buzz in my ears as I sit, my gear feeling more like shackles than armor. The idea of leaving... it's like someone's suggesting I cut off my own limb.

"Guys, come on, let's not jump the gun here," I try to interject, but even my voice sounds distant, hollow. The words don't carry the conviction I need them to have. Not when my brain is spinning faster than a puck in overtime.

No one replies. The silence is theirs, now. Eyes on the floor, I'm trying to ignore the clench of my gut, the racing of my heart. Leaving? I can't fathom it. This team, this city—it's become a part of me. But the chance to move up, to maybe one day hoist that cup... it's tempting, a siren song luring me toward jagged rocks.

"Hey, you sure you're alright, man?" Marco claps a hand on my shoulder, grounding me for a moment in the sea of chaos. He's the only one talking to me now, I guess.

I reply automatically, a half-hearted attempt at keeping things normal. "Just got a lot on my mind."

"Understatement of the year," he replies dryly, but there's no humor in his eyes now—just shared worry.

"Guys, focus!" Coach's voice slices through the tension. "We got a game to win. We'll deal with... everything else later."

"Right," I echo, though inside, I'm anything but focused. My thoughts are ricocheting between staying and going. Between the comfort of home and the allure of the unknown. But how can I be present when every second ticks by like it might be my last with this team? Every laugh, every cheer from the crowd, every slap of the stick against the ice—it could all be slipping through my fingers.

I plaster on the grin everyone expects from Ethan Scott, defenseman extraordinaire. But beneath the surface, my world's still quaking, and I'm left wondering if the ice beneath my feet will hold or crack wide open, swallowing me whole. And then, it hits me—if I leave the Sabres, I'll be leaving Lily.

There's no way I'll survive playing out this game. I'm counting the minutes until I can talk to her. She'll know what to do.

***

The door to the team meeting room swings open with a quiet creak, and she's there—Lily Morgan, looking like the only steady thing in a world that's suddenly tilting on its axis. I'm leaning against the wall, trying to seem casual, but my heart's pounding a relentless beat, echoing the chaos that's erupted since the news of my transfer came out. We have mere minutes during intermission, and I'm not sure I should even be away from the rink right now.

"Hey," I manage to say, my voice sounding raspier than usual.

"Hey, Ethan." Her smile doesn't quite reach her eyes, but it's warm, and it grounds me more than anything else right now. She's standing at the threshold, hesitating just a moment before stepping in, as if crossing some invisible line into the eye of the storm.

She's got this way of looking at you, green eyes unwavering, like she can see straight into your soul. Except right now, those eyes aren't dissecting me—they're full of something softer, kinder. It's almost like she can shoulder some of the burden just by being here, without needing to say a word.

"You wanted to talk?" Her voice cuts through the low murmurs around us, clear and certain.

“Yes," I reply, pushing away from the wall, eager for any anchor in the middle of this uncertainty.

We find a quiet corner away from the locker room side of the room, where the clamor fades into a dull roar. Lily leans back against the cool surface of the wall, arms crossed over her chest, the picture of composure. But when she looks up at me, there's no mistaking the concern etched into the lines of her face.

"I just want you to know that Thompson told me about the transfer offer. I can't imagine how difficult this must be for you," she says softly, her gaze holding mine.

Her words are a balm, soothing the raw edges of my frayed nerves. "Yeah, it's...a lot," I admit, rubbing the back of my neck.

Lily nods, her expression empathetic. "You've got the whole team behind you, whatever happens. And me too."

"Thanks, Lily." My voice breaks a little on her name because it means more than she might realize. This team is my family, and she's become a part of that—a vital one. "I don't want to let anyone down, especially not you guys."

"Hey, look at me," she says gently, stepping close and tilting my chin up with a finger so I'm forced to meet her eyes. "You won't. You're Ethan Scott, remember? Wherever you end up playing, you'll do great things. I believe in you."

"Means a lot coming from you," I confess, the words slipping out before I can stop them. There's a spark in her eye, a silent acknowledgment of something deeper between us.

"Good," she replies with a hint of her usual playful tone, bumping her shoulder against mine. "Now, go show them why you're irreplaceable, okay?"

"Okay," I echo, bolstered by her faith in me. As I head back into the fray, I know I can keep skating forward, no matter how uncertain the ice ahead.

***

Despite my mind being more at ease for now, the rink has never felt so hollow. Our blades carve the ice, normally a symphony of teamwork, now just a disjointed cacophony. Pucks slap against the boards with a desperation that echoes my own heartbeat—fast and erratic. The guys are trying to keep things normal, but each pass feels like we're all holding our breaths, waiting for the news on my transfer to drop like a puck at center ice.

"Head up, Scott!" Marco barks from across the rink, his voice breaking through my reverie. I snap to attention, catching the puck on my stick and weaving through the cones with more force than finesse. My teammates' eyes follow me, an unspoken pact that they've got my back—yet each look feels like a quiet goodbye.

"Stay sharp," Marco chides gently. I can tell he's trying to lighten the mood, but even his usual spark is dimmed by the shadow of uncertainty hanging over us.

"Doing my best," I reply, forcing a grin that doesn't quite reach my eyes. We finish the play, and I skate free, feeling the weight of a hundred games, a thousand practices, and countless memories tethering me to this place.

The game drives on. The metallic clink of puck against post resonates through the rink, a sound that's both a taunt and a promise. I skate back to center ice, my blades cutting into the frozen surface with the precision of a well-rehearsed dance. The air is sharp in my lungs, that familiar cocktail of cold and exertion. I can smell the mix of sweat and rubber from the equipment—a scent as integral to hockey as the thrill of a sudden breakaway.

"Focus, Ethan," I mutter to myself, bending low for the face-off. Jamie winks at me from across the dot, the ever-present light in his eyes undimmed by our shared uncertainty.

The puck drops, and for a moment, there's only the game—my stick flexes under the force of my grip, the crowd roars like a wave crashing against the shore, and adrenaline surges through my veins. There's no room for doubt on the ice; it's all reaction, instinct, the pure joy of the play.

"Scott, left wing!" Lucas calls out, and I'm there, receiving his pass without a second's hesitation, darting past a defenseman with a move that's more muscle memory than conscious thought. My heart pounds in time with the staccato rhythm of skates and sticks, each beat a drumroll leading up to the climactic shot.

"Back to you!" I shout to Dylan, who's trailing just behind. He takes the puck and fires it home, a blur of motion that ends with the red light blazing.

"Nice assist!" he yells, throwing an arm around my shoulders as we skate back to our bench. But as the cheers of the fans wash over us, the weight of my potential transfer settles back onto my shoulders, heavier than before. It's not just about me—it's about every guy on this team, every fan in the stands, every moment we've shared on this ice. The cold is seeping into my bones, but it's a comforting chill—the kind that reminds me I'm alive, that I'm part of something as raw and beautiful as hockey.

And whether I stay or go, it's not just my legacy on the line—it's all of theirs, too.

CHAPTER TEN: MARCO

The cheers from the crowd still echo in my ears, a fading chorus as I push open the door to the locker room. Adrenaline courses through me, leaving my heart hammering against my ribs like it's trying to break out and take another victory lap around the rink. The game was a brutal dance on ice, as exciting as the years spent dodging cracks in inner-city rinks, the cold seeping into my bones but never cooling the fire within. But we had *won.*

I expect solitude, the quiet hum of fluorescent lights my only company, but there she is again—Lily Morgan, standing near the rink entrance, her presence an unexpected jolt to my senses. She keeps doing that. Surprise lights up her green eyes, those windows to a soul as fierce and passionate about hockey as any player who's ever set blade to ice. Her hair is pulled back, practical, no-nonsense. But there's something else tonight—a crackle in the air around her, anticipation that mirrors my own erratic pulse.

"Hey," I call out, my voice bouncing off the lockers, sounding too loud in the sudden stillness.

Her lips curve into that half-smile that always seems to know more than it lets on. It's disarming, the way she does that, turning my usual swagger into something less sure, more raw. I'm usually the one in control with women, the one who has the upper hand.

I can't help it; I start walking over to her, my skates leaving scuffs on the polished floor. Each stride feels charged, like I'm skating toward the goal with the puck on my stick during a power play. There's a magnetic pull—an invisible force field that Lily and I have been circling around ever since she waltzed into town with her plan to shake things up.

"Didn't expect to see you here," I say as I close the distance between us, my voice betraying none of the internal tumult her presence stirs within me.

"Neither did I," she replies, and there's laughter in her voice, a lightness that makes me want to lean in closer.

"Wild Shot" Silvestri doesn't get rattled easily, but Lily Morgan? She's the unexpected slap shot that slips past a goalie's guard—swift, precise, and impossible to ignore.

The adrenaline from the game is still doing laps around my veins as I stand here, inches away from Lily. Her sharp green eyes are locked onto mine, searching for something I'm not sure I want her to find. The dim light of the locker room throws shadows across her face, but it can't hide the flush of excitement on her cheeks or the way her chestnut hair tumbles in a perfect mess around her shoulders.

"Look, Lily," I start, and there's a hitch in my voice that feels like a puck to the gut. "I've gotta say, this whole... pretend thing we've got going on? I'm kind of—" I inhale sharply, feeling the words tumble out before I can stick-handle them into something smoother. "—enjoying it more than I thought I would."

Her eyes widen, as if I've just scored a top-shelf goal and she's the netminder who didn't see it coming. Her lips part slightly, and it's like I can hear the echo of the crowd after a game-winning shot, the silence that follows the surprise.

"Marco..." She breathes my name, infusing it with something that sounds suspiciously like attraction, and it resonates against the cool metal of the lockers behind us.

I can feel the heat of the moment pressing in around us, warming the chilled air of the empty locker room. It's unnerving, how much I want to keep talking, to tell her everything that's been spinning through my mind every time our eyes meet across the rink or when we're alone like this.

But I hold back because Marco Silvestri doesn't spill his guts. He skates fast, lives faster, and keeps his plays close to his chest. Yet, here I am, teetering on the edge of a line I never planned to cross.

The thud of my heart against my chest is the only sound I can focus on as I lean in, narrowing the space between Lily and me until it's barely there. My hand lifts almost of its own accord, and the second my fingertips brush against her cheek, I swear I can feel a current pass through us. Her skin is soft, but firm.

"Marco..." Her voice is barely above a whisper this time, and I'm not sure if she's questioning me or urging me on.

"Shh," I hush her gently, not wanting words to clutter this moment that feels as pivotal as a game in overtime. This isn't a guy who lives for the spotlight making a calculated move; this is me, Marco Silvestri, stripped of pretense and driven by something raw and real.

My thumb caresses the apple of her cheek, marveling at the warmth there. It's intimate, this touch, more than any late-night party flirtation or rink-side jest. It's the kind of touch that I hope she knows is true tenderness, and for a guy who's spent his life dodging vulnerability like a puck to the face, it feels revolutionary.

Her breath catches—so slight I might have missed it if I wasn't so tuned into her every reaction. And then, my lips are on hers, a cautious contact that belies the restless energy thrumming through me. For a heartbeat, we're both motionless, like that sacred pause before the puck drops and the whole world explodes into action.

But then, something shifts, and the kiss deepens with an intensity that blindsides me. It's no longer a soft exploration but a fevered declaration, a silent acknowledgement that whatever game we started with our pretend relationship has morphed into something neither of us can control anymore. Lily's lips are insistent against mine, telling me without words that she's as caught up in this as I am.

For a guy who prides himself on reading women, on playing them, I'm shockingly unprepared for the passion that overtakes me. But like any good player—and by that, I mean a player of hearts—I adapt quickly, matching her urgency with my own, losing myself in the sensation of her mouth moving with mine.

The taste of victory still lingers on my tongue, but it's nothing compared to the taste of Lily. Her kiss is unexpected and thrilling in its precision. The sweetness of her lips mingles with the salt on my skin, a flavor that's uniquely ours in this stolen moment.

I'm not sure where the player ends and the man begins anymore. Each second that our lips move together blurs that line further, until I can't tell if I'm Marco "Wild Shot" Silvestri scoring the winning goal or just Marco, the guy who can't get enough of this girl. The way her body presses into mine feels like she's slotting into place, like a puzzle piece I didn't know was missing. How can something feel so right and yet be born from pretense?

Her hair brushes against my cheek as we shift, finding a new rhythm together. The scent of her shampoo—a hint of vanilla and something wild, like the forest after rain—fills my senses, grounding me in the here and now, in the reality that is Lily Morgan. Her lips are soft and pliant against mine, igniting a fire within me that I never knew existed. It's like we're connected by an invisible thread, each touch sending sparks through my body.

Her fingers tangle in my hair as our kiss deepens, and I am completely lost in her. Every touch, every movement is like a symphony playing between us, and I never want it to end. I hold her face in my hand, relishing the way she responds to my touch.

I don't want to stop, I don't want to slow down. Because kissing her just physical pleasure; it's connecting with someone on a deeper level, finding a kindred spirit And as we continue to kiss, I know that this is where I belong – in this moment with her. The Kiss Cam has nothing on this—nothing on the seismic shift happening in my chest as I press her closer, our bodies a tangle of need.

"God, Lily," I murmur against her mouth, the words slipping out before I can cage them. My heart's slamming against my ribs, playing a rhythm wilder than any game buzzer. There's an honesty in this closeness that frightens me, a genuine pull that goes beyond our ruse, beyond the strategy of public affection we've been using to boost her marketing campaigns.

She's fire and fight, all wrapped up in the strength of a slap shot, and damned if I don't want to be on her team for more than just the publicity. Is it possible that I've found something worth more than the thrill of scoring on the ice?

Lily's breath catches, her body quivering against mine, and I feel her heart pounding alongside my own, the synchrony of our pulse points like a metronome for this crazy dance we've started. I'm lost in the sensation of her, in the taste that's uniquely Lily.

We break apart, gasping for air as though we've both been underwater too long, our lungs desperate for the oxygen that seems only available when we're inches apart. Our eyes lock, saying what our ragged breaths cannot, the silence charged with the echo of our shared heartbeat.

"Wow," she whispers, her voice breathless but laced with a laugh.

"Understatement," I reply, trying to recapture my usual cockiness—but I'm pretty sure my grin betrays me. Her lips are swollen from our kiss, a red flag waved at my self-control, urging it to charge once more.

But then reality slams into me like a check against the boards. We're not just two people who got caught up in a moment; we're a strategic move in a much larger game—one where more than hearts might be the ultimate casualty. I stand there, the heat of Lily's breath still mingling with mine, her taste a ghost on my lips. My heart hammers against my ribs, each thud echoing the turmoil in my head. I take a step back, but it's like moving through wet cement—every inch away from her is a Herculean effort.

"Marco..." Her voice is a whisper, laced with confusion and something that sounds dangerous

"Sorry, I—" The words strangle in my throat as I lock eyes with her. There's so much I want to say, so much I should explain, but right now, all I can see is the longing mirrored in those green eyes that have seen straight through my façade from day one.

I turn abruptly, the sound of my skates thudding the locker room floor an inelegant symphony. I can't look back, can't give in to the urge to pull her into my arms again. If I do, I'll never let go.

The door slams shut behind me with a finality that echoes through the empty corridor. I lean against the cold concrete wall, trying to catch my breath, trying to catch my bearings. My fingers brush against my lips, half expecting them to burn at the touch.

What are we doing, Lily? What am I doing?

The kiss—it wasn't just a kiss. It was a confession, a revelation, a moment of raw truth wrapped in a lie we've been living. And God help me, I don't know if we can ever go back to the way things were. I don't know if I even want to.

"Get it together, Silvestri," I mutter to myself, pushing off the wall.

I walk, not knowing where I'm going, just moving to keep the storm inside me at bay. Every stride takes me further from her, but she's under my skin, in my blood, an indelible mark on whatever soul I've got left.

As the adrenaline from the game fades, replaced by a different kind of rush, I realize that this uncertain path we're on is more treacherous than any play on the ice. With Lily, it's not just about scoring or winning; it's everything else that comes after the buzzer—the silence, the emptiness, the fear of what happens when the crowd goes home and you're left wondering if any of it was real.

And damn it, I want it to be real.

But tonight, I've played the toughest game of my life, and for the first time, I'm scared of what I might lose.

CHAPTER ELEVEN: LILY

The frigid air bites at my cheeks as I hustle toward the community center, my breath misting in front of me like a smoky harbinger of the bustling day ahead. The weight of my warm coat feels comforting, almost protective against the early morning chill, and my boots crunch determinedly over the frost-kissed grass.

I'm here before anyone else, as is my habit, the sky still painted with the soft blush of dawn. I can't feel invigorated by the prospect of diving into today's projects. This is where I thrive, where my passion for hockey and community meshes into something tangible, something that can truly make a difference.

The community center looms before me, its brick facade welcoming in the golden hue of the rising sun. I push open the heavy door, stepping into the warmth that envelops me like an old friend's embrace. The scent of polished wood and freshly brewed coffee greets me, a familiar comfort.

"Morning, Lily!" Ethan's voice cuts through the quiet, his presence immediately filling the space with an energy that's contagious. I turn to find him approaching, his tall figure moving with the easy grace of an athlete, his sandy-blond hair tousled just enough to give him that effortless charm.

"Hey, Ethan," I reply. There's a spark in his bright blue eyes that mirrors my own excitement, and it sends a jolt of anticipation through me. We're about to dive into the thick of it, and having Ethan by my side makes it all seem like an adventure rather than work.

But as I smile back at Ethan, a pang of guilt twists in my stomach. Just last night, Marco's lips were on mine in a kiss so passionate it felt like it could ignite the very air around us. The memory sends a flush of warmth coursing through me, starkly at odds with the chill I've just escaped from outside. Marco, with his dark, tousled hair and those deep, mischievous eyes, fills my thoughts in a way I can't shake.

I glance at Ethan. He's everything stable and good. The contrast between him and Marco couldn't be more pronounced if it tried. The guilt gnaws at me more with each passing second. Here I am with

Ethan, ready to tackle the day's challenges together, while the echo of Marco's kiss still lingers on my lips. It feels like a betrayal, even though Ethan and I are nothing more than colleagues, friends working towards a common goal. But the way my heart races at the thought of Marco, and the undeniable chemistry between us, complicates everything.

I force a smile, pushing the guilt and confusion to the back of my mind. "Ready to get started?" I ask Ethan, hoping my voice doesn't betray the inner conflict I'm feeling.

"Absolutely," Ethan responds with a grin, his enthusiasm undimmed. He's ready to dive into the work, to make a difference in the community we both care so much about. And I want to be there with him, fully present and focused on the tasks at hand.

So I bury those thoughts, lock them away where they can't interfere with the work that needs to be done. Ethan deserves my full attention, and the community deserves my best effort. But as the day wears on, I know I'll have to confront these feelings to make sense of them before they consume me. For now, though, I focus on the here and now, on the work Ethan and I are doing together, and try to forget the kiss that changed everything.

"Looks like we've got our work cut out for us," I remark, a playful glint in my eye. I swipe a finger down the list, pausing at each task as if mentally checking them off before they're even done. "Okay. How about I take the sign-ups for the charity match and you handle equipment checks?" It seems fitting—me with the people and him with the gear. A balance of strengths.

"Sounds like a plan," Ethan agrees with a nod, his bright blue eyes scanning the list as well. "But are you sure you don't want to arm wrestle for it? You look like you could take me."

A chuckle escapes me before I can stop it. "In your dreams, Scott. Besides, we're about *engaging* the community, not scaring them away with our competitive streaks." I tap the paper lightly, setting our division of labor in stone.

"True," he says with a feigned sigh of defeat. "Although, I'd love to see you on the ice, Morgan. Bet you're fierce."

"Keep that up, and I might start thinking you're actually impressed by me," I tease back.

Ethan grins, and I swear I can almost see the rink reflected in his eyes. "Would that be so bad?"

"Depends on whether you can keep up."

"Challenge accepted." He winks, and we dive into our tasks.

The hours fly by, a blur of color and laughter as Ethan and I tackle the list of tasks that seem to have no end. The work is demanding, but his presence makes it lighter. There's something disarming about the way he listens—truly listens—his bright blue eyes never straying from mine when I speak, making me feel heard in a way I hadn't realized I was missing.

"Okay, so these flyers need to go up on all the main bulletin boards," Ethan says, handing me a stack with that easy smile of his. "I'll take the left hall, you take the right?

"Got it." I nod, feeling a warm glow at the simple task, knowing it's another small piece of the puzzle falling into place.

We split up, each covering different sections of the community center, and I notice how easily we divide and conquer. It's not just the work; it's the sense that we're a team now. I catch myself stealing glances at him when he's not looking, the way he moves with a grace that belies his powerful frame—a defender even off the ice. I wonder what Ethan would do if he didn't play hockey. He seems made for it.

Then, I wonder what Marco would do, and I could see his bravado and cockiness fitting in almost anywhere that flash and swagger are needed. He's bold, and fortune favors the bold.

But Ethan? His humility shines through in every interaction, every polite "please" and "thank you" to volunteers, every time he bends down to pick up a stray piece of trash without a second thought. Where will the world take him next year after he's done with his degree? I think of my dad, how sad he was after his injury took him out of the game—even though he tried to hide it, being without hockey changed him.

Later, as the afternoon light wanes, casting long shadows across the nearly empty hall, I find myself perched on the edge of a table, legs swinging slightly, while Ethan finishes gathering the last of the clipboards with players for the charity game.

"Hey, Ethan?" My voice echoes softly in the quiet space, and he turns, attentive.

"Yeah, Lily?"

I take a deep breath, feeling an inexplicable urge to share a piece of myself that's been locked away for too long. "Did I ever tell you about my dad's injury?"

His expression shifts to one of concern, the teasing glint in his eyes replaced by a gentle seriousness. "No, you didn't."

"Uh..." Suddenly, it feels like the walls are closing in, and I almost regret bringing it up. But Ethan's patient silence coaxes the words out of me. "He was a great player, could have gone pro. But during a game in his senior year, he took a bad hit—shattered his knee. Just like that, his career was over before it even started."

"Wow, Lily, I'm sorry to hear that," he replies, leaning against the wall opposite me.

"It's okay. It was a long time ago," I say, but the old ache flares up, familiar and sharp. "It's part of why I loved playing hockey in high school, you know? Felt like... like I was carrying on something important for him. He taught me everything about the game."

Ethan nods slowly, understanding dawning in his gaze. "That's a heavy mantle to carry, but it sounds like you played with a lot of heart."

"Too much sometimes," I admit with a small laugh, brushing a strand of hair behind my ear. "But it made me who I am today. Passionate, driven... maybe a little stubborn."

"Nothing wrong with a bit of stubbornness," he says with a grin, crossing the distance between us. "Especially when it's for something you love."

"Exactly." The word hangs between us, charged with an unspoken connection that has been building all day.

In this quiet moment, with the fading sunlight filtering through the windows and the empty echo of the community center around us, I realize just how comfortable I've become in Ethan's company. He doesn't push or pry; he simply accepts my vulnerability and offers his own strength in return.

And for the first time in what feels like forever, I allow myself to lean into that kindness, to acknowledge the flutter in my chest when he looks at me that way—like I'm more than just another teammate, more than just another project.

"Thanks for listening, Ethan," I say, my voice barely above a whisper.

"Anytime, Lily." His smile warms me more than any cup of hot chocolate ever could.

Ethan's broad shoulders slump forward as he exhales. The sight of him vulnerably hunched over, with that mop of sandy-blond hair falling into his eyes, strikes a chord in me. He runs a hand through his hair and glances out at the snowflakes that are now cascading down, blanketing the world in white. The snow is unexpected, a late spring blast of flurries that I was hoping would hold off until after our day's commitment.

"Your turn, huh?" I prompt gently. I focus on his face, waiting for him to open up as I did moments ago.

"You know, Lily," he starts, blue eyes locking onto mine with an intensity that makes my heart skip a beat, "this hockey gig... it's not just a game for me. It never was." He pauses, then continues. "My folks, they've always been all about discipline, about striving for excellence. Dad played college hockey, and well, there's this unspoken rule that I'm supposed to go further, aim higher."

"Pressure," I murmur, understanding more than he realizes. My own past, the weight of expectation, feels like a mirror to his confession.

"Exactly." Ethan leans back against the wall, the lines of tension around his eyes easing as he talks. "And I don't mind the hard work, you know? The early mornings, the late nights, the constant ache in my muscles—it's part of the deal. But sometimes, I just wonder what it'd be like to play without that heavy shadow looming over me."

"Freedom," I say softly.

"Freedom," he echoes with a wistful grin. He gazes out the window again, where the snowstorm has turned the world into a dizzy swirl of white. "Kinda like this storm. Wild, relentless, doing its own thing regardless of what anyone expects."

The cozy confines of the community center seem to grow even smaller, the walls inching closer as if to shelter us from the chaos outside. There's comfort in the shared silence, in the warmth that radiates from the heat vents above and from Ethan's presence beside me. I watch as the snow gathers in drifts against the glass, and for a moment, the rest of the world fades away until there's nothing but the two of us and the steady rhythm of falling snow.

"Thanks for sharing that, Ethan," I say after a beat, reaching out to place my hand over his. "It means a lot."

"Hey, we're in this together, right?" He gives my hand a gentle squeeze before letting go, and the simple gesture is enough to send a fresh wave of warmth coursing through me.

Together. The word resonates with a promise, a possibility of something new and thrilling blooming between us, despite the frosty tempest outside.

But what about Marco?

It's Marco's kiss that echoes in my mind, loud and clear. It was a spark, unexpected and searing, leaving a smoldering trail of confusion in its wake. The memory of his lips against mine sends a guilty shiver down my spine as I sit next to Ethan.

"Something else on your mind?" Ethan asks, his voice low, a touch of concern lacing his words.

"Nothing I can't handle," I lie smoothly, or as smoothly as I can muster. The truth is, I'm wrestling with a tangle of emotions, each one slippery and elusive.

"Okay, if you say so," he says, but the way he watches me, patient and attentive, tells me he's not entirely convinced.

Pushing aside thoughts of Marco—that kiss, the rush of adrenaline, the raw passion—I bring myself back to the now, to Ethan. He's been nothing but supportive. And I need to get out of my own head.

"Let's finish this up," I suggest, shaking off the last vestiges of doubt. "We can make sure we're all packed up and make a dash for the cars."

Ethan's answering grin is all the encouragement I need. Together, we gather and pack, our movements synchronized in an easy rhythm. As I pass him a folder with the sign-up forms, our fingers brush, and the spark is there—but it's different from the one Marco ignited. It's steadier, more enduring, like the glow of embers rather than a fleeting blaze.

I allow myself to enjoy the simple pleasure of Ethan's company. It's in these quiet moments that I notice how easily we move around each other, an unrehearsed choreography.

"Ready to brave the cold?" Ethan asks, offering me a hand with my heavy tote bag.

"Ready as I'll ever be," I answer, hoisting the strap over my shoulder. But as we head toward the exit, neither of us seems in a hurry to leave the sanctuary we've created.

At the door, we pause, and I feel the weight of his gaze on me before I even meet it. When I do, it's like skating into an unexpected hit—it knocks the breath right out of me. There's something in Ethan's eyes, a depth I hadn't noticed before, a silent question lingering in the air between us.

"Thanks for today, Ethan. Truly." The words come out softer than intended, laced with a sincerity that feels too raw, too revealing.

"Anytime, Lily." His voice is gentle, yet it resonates with something more, something unspoken that tugs insistently at the heartstrings I've been trying so hard to ignore.

We stand there, locked in a gaze that says more than words ever could, until the distant rumble of thunder reminds us of the world waiting outside. Reluctantly, I break away, the spell of the moment shattered by the reality of the storm. As I step out into the swirling snow, I pull my coat tighter around me, the chill of the air nothing compared to the confusion that swirls inside.

What am I doing? What is happening between Ethan and me? But there's no time for answers—not now. With one last glance at the warm glow spilling from the community center's windows, I head home, the flurries erasing my footsteps as quickly as they're made, like the doubts I'm desperately trying to leave behind.

Snowflakes dance in the glow of the streetlamps, each one a delicate whisper against the night sky. My boots crunch over the freshly fallen snow as I put distance between myself and the community center, where warmth and light still beckon from behind me. It feels like stepping out of one world and into another—the one where choices aren't just about charity events and who gets to untangle streamers.

My breath puffs out in white clouds, mingling with the frigid air, as I replay the day's events. Ethan's laughter, his teasing, those impossibly blue eyes that seem to look right through my defenses—it's all too much and not enough at the same time. There's an ease between us, a rhythm.

But then there's Marco. Passionate, fiery Marco, who doesn't just skate—he carves himself into the ice hard. His kiss... it was reckless, a shot aimed straight for the heart, and it left me reeling. I stop mid-stride, taking in the silent, snow-covered streets of my hometown. This is where I learned to love hockey, to stand strong, to fight for what I believe in. And now, here I am, caught up in a game I never saw coming—one with higher stakes than any championship.

What will it be? The steady flame that warms me slowly or the wildfire that consumes everything in its path? I'm alone with my thoughts, my doubts, and the two very different men who've managed to skate circles around my heart.

CHAPTER TWELVE: LILY

The cursor blinks at the end of my latest report, each line confirming the success I've been nurturing since I took over as head of marketing for the team. I lean back in my leather chair, allowing a slow smile to spread across my face. The numbers don't lie; attendance is up, social media engagement is through the roof, and merchandise sales are soaring like one of Marco's unexpected slapshots. Chestnut strands fall into my eyes as I shake my head in disbelief—looks like this small-town hockey aficionado might just have some serious game off the ice too.

"Numbers looking good, Lily?" Mr. Thompson's voice slices through my reverie as he peers over my shoulder with an expression that can't decide between pleased and perturbed.

"Better than good," I reply, pivoting in my seat in the conference room to face him squarely, my green eyes locking onto his. "We're on track for a record season attendance if we keep this up."

"Let's hope so." His gaze flits to the door just as it swings open, admitting a gust of air along with Krista—the icy blonde embodiment of ambition. Her piercing blue eyes scan the room like she's calculating how to buy it, sell it, or bulldoze it for something better.

"Hope is for amateurs," Krista announces, not bothering with greetings. She places a stack of folders on the conference table with a precision that mirrors her sharp bob haircut. "I prefer results."

"Which Lily has been delivering," Mr. Thompson points out, though his tone suggests he's throwing me a life preserver in shark-infested waters.

"Sure," Krista concedes with a saccharine smile, "if you consider cozying up to players professional. That fake dating stunt with Marco? Creative, I'll give you that. But it walks a fine line between innovative and inappropriate."

My heart clenches, but I mask it with a laugh. "Marco and I are just playing our parts to drum up interest. It's all about the narrative, Krista. You should understand that—it's Marketing 101."

"*Narrative*," she scoffs, rolling her eyes dramatically. "Right. Because nothing says 'team spirit' like manufactured romance."

"Actually, it does," I counter, standing up to my full height—which admittedly still leaves me craning my neck to meet her gaze. "It's about the human element. Fans eat that up. They want stories, connection. Not just cold, hard stats."

"Stories are for bedtime, Lily," Krista retorts, leaning forward with hands flat against the table, resembling a corporate predator ready to pounce. "And I'm not here to tuck our investors in at night. Or any of our players."

Mr. Thompson shifts uncomfortably, clearly feeling the temperature drop in the room. He's caught in the crossfire of a battle he never signed up to referee.

"Both of you have valid points," he interjects, trying to smooth the edges of the conversation. "But let's stay focused on the strategies that will bring us success."

"Of course, Mr. Thompson," I say, turning to flash him a reassuring smile. "That's all I'm focused on. Success for the team."

"Then let's hear what you both have to propose," he says with a finality that seals the room tighter than a goalie's net during playoffs.

Krista straightens, her eyes glinting with the promise of challenge, and I know that no matter how solid my numbers are, this is one game that's far from over.

The tension in the room is palpable, a living, breathing entity that coils around my throat and tightens with every word Krista utters. The meeting room, usually welcoming, now feels more like the gladiatorial arenas of old, where blood sport was business as usual. I'm just glad that this meeting is end-of-day. I couldn't stand walking on eggshells all day after this.

"Data-driven targeting will not only capture but engage our fanbase," Krista says, her voice echoing off the sterile white walls, the sleek glass table reflecting her confidence back at her. Her presentation clicks through slides faster than a puck flying across ice, each one more aggressive, more ambitious than the last.

"Imagine exclusive events with top-tier access to only select fans—and by that, I mean those who donate to the school endowment or can bring us high visibly. Wouldn't it be great to be leveraging social influencers with millions of followers?" she proposes, her icy gaze scanning me any sign of weakness, any hint of dissent.

I watch Mr. Thompson's brow furrow, his usual calm demeanor unsettled by the sheer audacity of the pitch. Beside him, the rest of the management team exchanges wary glances, their comfort with traditional methods clashing against the shiny lure of Krista's modern approach.

"Revenue projections indicate a spike within the first quarter alone," she concludes with a flourish that might have been impressive if it didn't feel like a slap to my face—a challenge to everything I've worked for. "We're wasting time groveling with the commoners to revive things. We need to aim for a more *socially elite* echelon."

A beat of silence follows, then another. It's deafening, this quiet before the storm, and it takes everything in me not to let my shock show. But I can't afford to look rattled, not when I've poured heart, soul, and countless hours into building something genuine for the team.

"Interesting," I hear myself say, my voice steadier than I feel. Her head snaps toward me, those piercing eyes trying to skewer me in place. But I'm already moving—metaphorically at least—adapting to this unexpected play like I've done on the ice a thousand times before.

"However," I continue, leaning forward, "Our fanbase isn't just a series of data points to be exploited, nor will you find the heart of hockey in the upper crust. The fans are real people who crave real connections. My strategy builds those relationships. It nurtures them."

There's strength in my words, born from years of being underestimated and fighting to earn my place. This isn't just about defending a position; it's about proving that integrity and passion have a spot in this game too.

"Krista's plan is... flashy," I concede, acknowledging the elephant in the room without giving it room to charge. "But hockey's about more than flash. It's about heart, community, and, yes, even tradition. We risk alienating our core supporters if we pivot too hard, too fast. I don't want to exclude high rollers—we'll take those, too!"

The room chuckles collectively.

"But the people you seem to disdain are what makes hockey *hockey*, Krista. We can't cast them aside."

I stand my ground, knowing that now, more than ever, my ability to think on my feet—to navigate corporate rivalry—is crucial. Not just for my career but for the soul of the team. And as the management team nods thoughtfully, murmuring agreements and considerations, I can feel the tide shifting beneath us all. Maybe, just maybe, the game isn't over yet.

She smirks her blue eyes like shards of ice aimed directly at my confidence. "Lily, darling, we're not just in your quaint hometown anymore. This city has grown in the last five years, and this is big-league marketing; we aim for impact, not comfort."

"Big-league marketing doesn't have to be impersonal," I counter. "We've seen a significant increase in season ticket holders since implementing community-focused initiatives. Fans want to feel part of the team's journey, not just spectators to it."

Krista leans back, flicking an imaginary speck of dust off her tailored blazer. "And yet, the potential reach of a more... aggressive high-class, digital strategy could dwarf those numbers."

"*Could*," I emphasize. "Or it could backfire. Our demographic values authenticity. My approach cultivates that."

"Authenticity is just another buzzword these days," she dismisses with a wave of her hand.

I clench my jaw, forcing myself to maintain composure. Krista is good, no doubt about it. But so am I. I know this game—both on the ice and in the boardroom—and I'm not about to let her check me into the boards without a fight.

"Perhaps," I concede, "But in the end, it's not just about buzzwords or even numbers. It's about loyalty. And loyalty isn't bought with flash; it's built with trust."

A murmur of approval rises from the management team, and I allow myself a small, internal victory lap. The tension in the room is still palpable, a playoff-level intensity that's both exhilarating and exhausting.

"Trust is important, Lily, but so is innovation," Krista counters, her cool gaze fixed on me. "We can't afford to stagnate."

"Of course," I agree, nodding to acknowledge her point while internally bracing for the next volley. "Innovation drives us forward, but it shouldn't leave our foundation behind. We can introduce new ideas while still honoring what our fans love about hockey—the grit, the passion, and the sense of family."

"Your sentimental approach is charming, but charm doesn't fill arenas," she says sharply, her voice rising.

"Actually, Krista, it does," I shoot back, the muscles in my shoulders tensing as if I'm ready to block a shot. My own voice rises, too. "Because charm translates to fan engagement, and engaged fans are loyal fans."

"Enough," Mr. Thompson interjects, his voice cutting through the debate. "Both of you make compelling arguments. We'll take some time to review the strategies further."

I nod, schooling my features into a mask of professional gratitude. As the meeting dissolves and the others file out, I sit for a moment longer, trying to catch my breath. My heart pounds against my ribs—a muffled drum reminding me of the stakes. I've held my own against Krista's onslaught today, but the question lingers in the back of my mind, heavy and unrelenting: Will it be enough?

Back in the privacy of my office, I close the door and lean back against the cool wood, letting out a breath I didn't know I was holding. My gaze drifts to the framed photo on my desk—me as captain, hoisting the championship trophy my senior year, surrounded by my teammates. Their faces are alight with joy, with victory. We did that together. But now, it feels like I'm skating solo, trying to dodge body checks from someone who's supposed to be on my side.

My phone buzzes—it's Marco. My stomach flips as I swipe to read the text, which simply says: *Pizza?*

CHAPTER THIRTEEN: MARCO

The dim glow of the laptop screen is the only source of light that fights against the darkness in the room, casting long shadows across the scattered papers that litter the table. I lean back in my chair, rubbing my tired eyes as I try to focus on the strategy laid out before us. Lily is next to me, scanning the latest stats with an intensity that's both admirable and slightly intimidating.

When I'd said *pizza,* I had meant at a cozy Italian restaurant, with wine and close quarters. Not that I would be bringing a pie to her office because she'd gotten laser-focused on work.

"Can you believe Krista?" Lily huffs, her voice laced with frustration as she shuffles through the documents. "She thinks she can just steamroll over everyone with her tactics."

I snort, imagining Krista's icy blue stare, so confident and calculated. Lily's right; Krista's shenanigans are becoming more brazen by the day. "She's like a bulldozer in heels. No subtlety whatsoever," I comment, trying to keep the atmosphere light despite the gravity of our situation.

Lily chuckles, and the sound warms the chilly room. "Well, she hasn't met the immovable object that is Lily Morgan," she declares, her thick hair falling over her shoulder as she leans forward, her gaze never leaving the papers. She's all fiery determination, and it's damn impressive.

I watch her for a moment, the way her brows knit together in concentration, the way her lips move silently as she reads. There's something about Lily, something that makes you want to be better just by being near her. It's in the way she carries herself. It pulls at something deep inside me—a longing I've kept buried.

"Marco?" Lily turns toward me, her expression softening when she catches the intensity of my stare. "You okay? You've been quiet. And, thanks for the pizza, if I didn't say that. Sorry."

"Ah, yeah. No, you did say it. And you're always welcome." I clear my throat, suddenly aware of how close we are sitting. The air feels thick, heavy with unspoken words. I hesitate, feeling the weight hanging between us like a shadow. Do I dare let her in? Can I trust her with the parts of me I've fought so hard to hide?

"Actually, there's something I've been meaning to talk about," I start, and even to my own ears, my voice sounds more serious than usual. I take a deep breath, steadying myself. "It's about my past."

Her expression shifts from concern to curiosity. "Your past?"

"Yeah." I swallow hard, unsure of where to begin. This isn't something I share lightly, but if there's anyone who might understand, it's Lily. She's seen the rough edges of life, knows what it's like to fight for something more. "Things weren't always easy for me growing up."

I lean forward, elbows resting on the cluttered table that's become our makeshift command center, and I feel the intensity of Lily's gaze, patient and expectant. It's strange—here in this dim room, with the glow of our laptops casting long shadows, I find myself ready to unravel my story for her.

"Growing up," I begin, my voice steady despite the storm of memories brewing inside, "home was... well, it wasn't the safe, comforting place people usually talk about." I pause, choosing my words carefully. "Every day felt like skating on thin ice, never knowing when it would crack."

Lily doesn't speak, but I can see it in her eyes—she's here with me, not just in this room, but she's stepping into the chaos of my past, willing to understand the game that saved me from that life. Her sharp green eyes, always so full of fire on the ice, now reflect a softness, a warmth that encourages me to continue.

Lily's hand inches closer to mine, almost touching but not quite. Her presence is grounding, giving me the courage to peel back the layers I've clung to for protection. As I open up to her, I can feel the walls I've built around myself starting to crumble. And for the first time, I'm not sure I mind.

"Hockey was my safe zone, you know? The rink was the one place where the noise of my parents' fights couldn't reach me. Where I could be more than just 'that kid from the rough part of town.'"

I notice her body leaning in slightly, an almost protective stance, as if she's ready to defend me from my own personal history. She's always been a fierce advocate on the ice; now, I see that same tenacity directed toward understanding me.

"Every goal, every check against the boards—it wasn't just about the game. It was me... fighting for something else. For a chance at a different life." My hands move animatedly.

"Marco..." Lily finally speaks, her voice laced with a depth of empathy that matches the complexity of our late-night planning sessions. "The successes you've had—they're proof of how much heart you put into everything. Not just hockey."

Her words are validating. And in this moment, sharing my story with Lily, I feel like I'm more than just Marco "Wild Shot" Silvestri, the hotshot forward. I'm a person with a past that shaped me, but a future that's no longer set in stone.

As I reveal more of the gritty details—the skipped meals, the borrowed and secondhand gear, the endless hours of practice outside of any real rink—I see something shift in her. Lily Morgan, the girl who grew up breathing hockey just like me, understands the weight of dreams on young shoulders. As I recount those days where every slapshot was a plea for escape, my voice catches. It's not often that I let the dam break, that I allow the memories to flood back.

"Sometimes," I admit, my voice trembling like a loose puck on ice, "I'd sleep in my skates because they were the one thing that felt right. Like they were part of me and I wasn't just some kid trying to dodge the crap life threw my way."

I glance away from Lily, focusing on the scattered papers between us. They seem so trivial now, these strategies and schemes, when compared to the game of survival I've been playing all my life. I'm laid bare, stripped of my usual bravado like hockey gear tossed aside after a grueling match.

There's a gentle pressure on my arm then, and I look down to see Lily's hand resting there, her touch a lifeline. Her fingers are warm, grounding, and I'm keenly aware of her next to me—not just as the optimistic marketing whiz but as someone who sees beyond the facade.

She doesn't say anything, and she doesn't need to. That hand on my arm speaks volumes, conveying a silent promise that she's here with me in this dimly lit room where past and present collide. It tells me she's not just hearing my words; she's listening to the unspoken language of my faltering heart.

I take another deep breath, the kind that rattles your ribs as it goes down. The quiet in the room is so dense you could slice it with a skate blade. I've already opened up more than I intended, but Lily's hand on my arm steadies me like an anchor, and before I know it, I'm diving deeper into memories I usually keep locked away.

"Back when I was ten" —I start, forcing a half-smile— "I scored my first hat trick with the school team. Everyone was cheering, you know? But when I looked up at the stands... my old man wasn't there."

Her fingers tighten slightly on my arm, urging me to continue. It's a strange comfort, one I didn't realize I'd been craving until now.

"Turned out he got drunk and passed out in the street. Cops scooped him up and threw him in jail to dry out. He missed the whole game." My voice is casual, but the disappointment of that day still nips at me like the cold wind on the outdoor rinks where I learned to skate. "That's when I figured out that if I wanted something in this life, it was on me to make it happen."

As I share these pieces of my childhood, I feel a shift in the person sitting next to me. No longer just the girl who flirts with me at meetings or watches me play hockey from the stands. This is a new version of her, one who listens and understands, and it makes me want to tell her everything.

"It was tough," I admit, feeling the weight of her empathy in my chest. "But hockey was always my escape, my way to make sense of the world without him. And you get it, too, right?" I ask, searching her face for confirmation. "Hockey means something different to us. It's not just a game."

"Exactly," she responds quietly. In this small room with its dim lighting, it feels like we're in our own little world. The only things that exist are our words and emotions, hanging heavy in the air.

I've always played hockey like I live my life—fast, impulsive, with a touch of recklessness. It's worked for me so far, kept me from getting tripped up by things like fear or doubt. But as I sit across from Lily, the realization hits me—I might be falling for her. She's everything my chaotic upbringing wasn't—steady, passionate, driven by something pure and good. And I find myself wanting to be a part of that, to be more than just 'Wild Shot' Silvestri, the guy who scores on the ice but can't seem to score a genuine connection off it.

"You're a complicated guy, Wild Shot." Her use of my nickname sends a thrill through me, a reminder of the world where I am most confident, yet right now, I am anything but.

"Maybe," I say, because admitting that I am seems too raw, too real. But I lean closer to her, and the tension ratchets up a notch. We're close, so close I can see the flecks of gold in her green eyes, feel the warmth radiating from her skin.

I should pull back, put some professional distance between us, but instead, I find myself leaning in more, shrinking the space that divides our worlds. I remember every detail of kissing her, and I want to do it again. My breath mingles with hers, and there's this electric sensation that makes my heart hammer against my ribs.

"Marco..." she whispers, almost a warning, but she doesn't push me away.

"Sorry," I whisper back, not sure if I'm apologizing for getting too close or for wanting to get closer still. Her lips parted slightly, and it's like I'm under a powerful spell. It's a charged moment of intimacy, the kind that could change the course of everything between Lily and me. Lily's breath is a soft hush against my cheek, a counterpoint to the erratic pounding of my heart. Time has reduced to these moments between pulses, each second stretched and taut.

"Marco," she says again, her voice a delicate tremor that vibrates through the space between us. Her eyes lock onto mine, those sharp green pools reflecting a storm of emotions I can't quite decipher.

"Sorry," I mumble. This time, it's because I get what she's saying.

Back off.

It was weak—a penalty box-worthy play—and I'm cursing myself for not having the finesse I possess on the ice. But there's something about Lily that scrambles my defense, sends me into overtime without any clear strategy.

"Can we just..." She trails off, her gaze darting away. "Forget the kiss happened?"

I lean back. The chill from the void where our warmth once mingled hits me. "Yeah, of course." The lie tastes bitter on my tongue. We both know you can't un-score a goal.

"Should we call it a night?"

"Probably best," I agree, though every muscle protests the retreat. I help her gather the papers, maintaining a careful distance, as if she's surrounded by an invisible crease I dare not cross.

"Thanks for the help," she says, her tone professional but with an undercurrent I can't quite read. "I'll see you at the rink tomorrow."

"Sure thing, coach," I reply, aiming for a lighthearted quip but landing somewhere closer to desolation. She smiles, but it doesn't reach her eyes, and a part of me wonders if I've been benched in more ways than one.

Lily leaves, taking the light with her, and I'm left in the dim aftermath, haunted by what-ifs and might-have-beens. Was it opening up that pushed her away—or the lean in? As I pack away my own laptop, the silence looms, unanswered questions hanging in the air like the echo of a puck slamming against the boards. What will Lily do? Will she ever look at me the same way after tonight?

CHAPTER FOURTEEN: LILY

The moment I step into the chilled embrace of the hockey arena, my heart skips with a familiar cocktail of excitement and anxiety. It's game day, another test of wills on ice, another chance for triumph or heartache. My breath comes out in visible puffs, mingling with the scent of cold steel and anticipation that permeates the air.

From the sidelines, I lean against the barrier, my eyes scanning over the team as they warm up. Their movements are fluid and precise, each stride on the ice deliberate, every stretch and drill performed with an intensity that showcases deep concentration. It's a dance I know well, one that's etched into muscle memory from years spent gripping a stick rather than a marketing portfolio.

I feel the energy coursing through the rink, electric and unyielding, reflecting off their determined faces. These players, they're not just athletes; they're gladiators gearing up for battle, and it's my job to ensure the world sees the heroes I see. My hair slips from behind my ear, a loose strand fluttering before my eyes, but I barely notice. I'm too caught up in the rhythm of skates slicing the ice, pucks thudding against the boards, the language of hockey that I've been fluent in since childhood.

My fingers tighten around the railing, the cool metal biting into my palms. These men, this team—they carry more than just the hopes of fans; they bear the weight of legacy, of dreams deferred, much like my father's all those years ago. And yet, despite the pressure, they wear their resolve like armor, ready to clash and conquer.

And just like them, I have a role to play, a contribution to make. They rely on strength and skill; I rely on strategy and spirit. Together, we're a force, and as the arena slowly fills with the buzz of an expectant crowd, I let their energy seep into my bones. Today, like every game day, we stand united, chasing victory on ice slick with promise and peril. And I wouldn't have it any other way.

Skates carve into the ice with a satisfying scrape, and my eyes are drawn to the fluidity of Ethan's movements. He's poetry in motion, darting forward with an agility that belies his broad-shouldered frame.

His jersey ripples with each stride, bright blue eyes fixed on the puck as if nothing else in the world exists. It's like watching someone born to do exactly this—defend, protect, lead. I feel my heart skip a beat, an involuntary reaction.

"Watch the hips, not just the puck," I whisper under my breath, recalling my dad's old advice. The athlete in me appreciates Ethan's finesse; the woman in me can't ignore the surge of attraction that pools in my stomach. In another life, he could've been a dancer. But here, on the ice, Ethan is in his element, and it's impossible not to admire him.

The sharp sound of another blade biting the ice pulls me from my reverie, and my gaze shifts across the rink. Marco—Wild Shot—lives up to his moniker, puck on his stick as though magnetized, dark hair tamed beneath his helmet. He moves with a different kind of grace—confident curves that are as much a part of him as the stick in his hands. His deep brown eyes catch mine, and for a heartbeat, the intensity there makes everything else fade away.

He's all raw passion and calculated risks, a contrast of shadow and fire against the stark white of the arena. There's something about the way Marco holds himself, commands attention without demanding it, that sets my pulse racing. On the ice, he's untamed energy harnessed for a singular purpose—to dominate, to score, to win. Off it, well, that's a whole other game, one that I'm both intrigued and wary of playing.

Last night, after Marco shared those raw, painful parts of his past with me—the abuse that shadowed his childhood, the battles he's fought to stand where he is today—I felt a shift. The revelation was a heavy weight. Pulling away from him afterward felt like the only thing I could do, yet it was the hardest choice I've ever made. In that moment, Marco wasn't just the confident player with a penchant for mischief; he was vulnerable, real in a way that scared me.

Now, watching him glide across the ice, I'm torn. That same vulnerability that made me step back also pulls me closer, a magnetic force rooted in a desire to understand him, to peel back the layers and see the man beneath the persona. Yet, I'm cautious, aware that stepping back into his orbit could mean getting burned by the very fire that drives him.

His gaze holds mine across the distance, a silent acknowledgment of everything that's passed between us. There's an unspoken question there, a challenge: can I handle the depth, the complexity of who he is? The truth is, I don't know. But the pull I feel towards him, intensified by his honesty, is something I can't easily dismiss. I'm beginning to see

Marco Silvestri not just as a love interest or a teammate, but as a person with a story that's both tragic and triumphant.

As they continue their pre-game rituals, Ethan and Marco are oblivious to the storm they stir within me. Here I am, caught in the crossfire of admiration and desire, wondering which flame burns brighter.

The air horn blares, slicing through the charged atmosphere of the arena. I'm on the edge of my seat as players dash across the ice, a flurry of color against the shimmering white. The game has begun, and with it, an internal battle in the confines of my chest.

"Come on, Ethan!" I hear myself yell as he intercepts a pass with seamless precision, his broad shoulders pivoting as he sends the puck gliding to a teammate. Cheering for him feels like backing the underdog, the unsung hero—except Ethan Scott is anything but unnoticed on this team.

But then, Marco takes possession. He's a meteor streaking down the ice, leaving defenders trailing in his wake. And when he slams the puck into the net, the crowd erupts, and so does my heart. For a moment, I forget to breathe, captivated by his raw talent. The scoreboard changes, and I jump to my feet, clapping before I can stop myself.

"Marco! Yes!" I shout, the excitement spilling from me unbidden. My voice blends with the chorus of cheers, but inside, I'm a discordant note—a clash of loyalties that muddies the harmony.

As the game progresses, the intensity ramps up notch by brutal notch. Ethan sets up a play, sacrificing a shot at glory to assist a rookie in scoring his first goal. The pride in his eyes is evident even from this distance, and it pulls at me, the power of selflessness.

Yet, each time Marco nears the puck, anticipation is in the air, a collective holding of breaths for what magic he might conjure next. His confidence is infectious, and I find myself leaning forward, yearning to see what he'll do. My loyalty flickers between them like a puck ricocheting off the boards—back and forth, never settling. By the end of the second period, I'm emotionally wrung out. I applaud Ethan's assists, my chest swelling with pride at his camaraderie. Moments later, I'm swept up in the thrill of Marco's relentless pursuit of victory, his celebrations igniting something wild within me.

"Who are you rooting for?" a fan asks beside me, but I can't answer. How can I choose? Ethan, or Marco?

I don't have an answer. Not yet.

As the final period unfolds, I'm no closer to a decision than when I started. But one thing is clear—I'm playing a game that's far more complicated than anything happening on the ice. And I think that both Ethan and Marco might be playing the same game, too.

Then it happens—just as the game is winding down, tensions high, Ethan blocks a shot that would have certainly found its way past our goalie. The whistle blows, signaling a stop in play, and suddenly, there's a commotion by the bench. I lean forward, straining to see what's happening.

Marco is standing from the bench, yelling at Ethan. I can't make out everything, but shouted words filter through.

Showing off for her...

"Are you serious right now, Silvestri?" Ethan's voice slices through the din of the arena, sharp and accusing. I'm out of my seta and jogging toward the box.

"I get it, man. But watch yourself. All is fair in love and hockey, Scott," Marco retorts with a sneer.

"*Love?* Is that what you call it?" Ethan's words are laced with sarcasm, but there's an edge to them that sends a chill down my spine. "What do all the girls you parade in and out of your bedroom call it?"

"Guys, don't—" I start, but my voice is lost in the chaos.

"Stay out of it, Morgan!" they both snap in unison, and I flinch at the vehemence in their tone. The two are in each other's faces now, helmets butting.

The referees and teammates manage to separate them before things escalate further, but the damage is done. They're both benched for the remaining minutes, leaving the ice thick with tension. I watch helplessly as the team rallies without them, securing the win in a flurry of plays.

As the final buzzer sounds, victory should feel sweet, but it's tainted with the bitter aftertaste of conflict. Their argument hangs heavy in the air, clouding the celebration. The rest of the team is elated, but I can barely muster a smile, my gaze flickering between Ethan and Marco as they skate past me.

"Great game," I try to say, but it sounds hollow, even to my own ears.

They both nod stiffly, their expressions unreadable. I'm left standing there, feeling cold despite the warmth of the arena, my mind a whirlwind of confusion. How did cheering for two incredible players become such a battleground?

CHAPTER FIFTEEN: ETHAN

The puck slides across the ice, a slick promise of victory as it meets Marco's stick. I'm perched on the bench, watching him weave through the defenders with the kind of grace that would have ballet dancers taking notes. Marco's been on fire lately, each game another notch in his belt, and another reason for scouts to keep their eyes peeled. This game is no different.

I lean forward, elbows resting on my knees, as he fakes left—no, right—and then snaps the puck straight into the net. The arena erupts into a cacophony of cheers, and despite the lingering sting of our recent spat, I feel a swell of pride. The scoreboard flashes the new tally, and I catch myself grinning like an idiot.

"Did you see that?" I turn to one of the rookies, whose eyes are wide with the same mix of awe and envy I've felt before.

"Wild Shot strikes again," he says, and we both chuckle.

"Wild" is an understatement. Since our argument, Marco's been playing like someone lit a rocket beneath him. His speed has notched up to a blur; his precision is surgical. But most impressive is how he reads the game—sees plays unfolding before anyone else does, like some hockey oracle. He's racking up goals and assists, becoming the linchpin of the team's offense.

As the buzzer signals the end of the period, I'm hit with a twinge of regret. We haven't really talked since the argument, just the necessary exchanges on the ice. Watching him now, I realize how much I miss shooting the breeze with him off the rink—his mischievous quips, the way he'd arch an eyebrow when he knew he was pushing my buttons.

Sean, our goalie, lifts his mask, revealing a grin that could outshine the arena's lights. There's a newfound energy buzzing through the team, a sense of unity that feels electric. Through every check into the boards, every power play, every heart-stopping save, our momentum surges. We're no longer just a team; we're a force. I see it in the focused set of my teammates' jaws, hear it in the rallying cries before we hit the ice.

Next period flies by. The puck shoots across the ice like a comet, and I'm the only one positioned to intercept it. My skates carve into the rink as I lean forward, my muscles tensing, ready for the burst of speed

I've been perfecting all season. The metallic scent of cold ice fills my nostrils, the roar of the crowd fades to a distant drumming in my ears—it's just me and the puck, destined to collide.

"Scott! Left wing!" I hear Marco's voice cut through the cacophony, crisp and clear.

I flick my wrist, sending the puck slicing through the air, landing perfectly onto Marco's tape. He takes it in stride, barreling down the left side. I don't need to look to know he'll make the shot; we've done this dance a hundred times in practice. My anticipation builds as I watch him close in on the net, then with a snap of his stick, the puck is behind their goalie, slamming against the twine.

"Score!" The announcer's bellow sends a surge of adrenaline through my veins. Our bench erupts, gloves slapping against pads, helmets clashing in boisterous celebration.

"Great pass, Ethan!" Marco skates up to me, his grin wide enough to span the rink. "You're on fire, man!"

"Thanks," I reply, bumping his fist with mine. "We're not letting up. This is our game."

As I skate back to my position, I can feel the weight of responsibility tethered to my jersey. Each game feels more pivotal than the last, each shift a chance to leave my mark. It's not just about me anymore; it's about us, this team that's become an extension of myself.

We win the faceoff, and I'm back on defense, eyes scanning for breaks, sticks, and the stray puck looking to sneak past me

"Keep it up, Ethan! You're leading us to the promised land!" Coach yells from the bench, every word punctuated by the staccato clap of his hands against the boards.

I nod, acknowledging his faith in me, and turn my attention back to the game. Every check I throw, every puck I block, it's all contributing to the momentum that's been building.

"Solid D, Scotty!" Lily hollers from the stands, her voice threading through the cheers and finding its way to me. Even without looking, I can picture her there—eyes sparkling, smile wide, wrapped in her varsity scarf.

The fight with Marco—no denying it was jealousy over my spending time with her.

Focus, Ethan! I chastise myself. There's time for romance after the buzzer.

The final minutes are a blur of motion. When the horn sounds, signaling the end of the game, we're still ahead. The scoreboard glows with our victory, another step closer to the championship we've all dreamed of.

"Way to dig deep, boys!" I tell my teammates in the locker room, clapping them on the shoulders. "Every shift counts, and you guys brought it all."

"Couldn't have done it without your lead," one of my linemates says, and I feel a swell of pride.

"Let's keep this fire burning," I say, meeting each of their gazes. "We've got more games to win, and I know we've got the grit to do it."

"Championship, here we come!" they echo back, and for a moment, all the uncertainties fade. We're unstoppable. And there's Marco at the center of it all, his performance guiding us forward. I can't shake the feeling that this season—this chance—is something special. And I'll be damned if I let anything, even old arguments or bruised egos, stand in the way of what we're building here.

***

"Great game today, Scott!" one of the rookies calls out he leaves the locker room, slapping my shoulder in camaraderie.

"Thanks," I manage, offering a tight smile. The praise feels hollow when I know that any game could be my last with the team that has become my family. The offer for a transfer still sits heavy in my locker, a simple piece of paper that holds the power to unravel everything. As I peel off my gloves, the weight of eyes on me is palpable. The news has spread like wildfire through the team.

"Is it true?" Sean's voice comes from beside me. Concern is etched across his brow. "You're considering a transfer?"

I meet his gaze, the familiar blue of the locker room suddenly feeling foreign. "I haven't decided anything yet."

"Man, you can't leave us now—not when we're this close," he presses, and I hear the unspoken plea for reassurance.

"Nothing's set in stone," I say, but it rings hollow even to my own ears. My heart is here, with these walls, these faces, but ambition is a siren's call that's hard to ignore.

"Hey, if it's a good opportunity, you gotta do what's best for you," Marco chimes in from across the room, his tone light but eyes sharp, studying me.

"Appreciate it," I reply carefully, though his words do little to ease the knot in my chest. Marco knows the stakes, and I'm suspicious of his well-wishes.

"Guys, let's not jump the gun," Coach interjects, his voice carrying the calm authority that always seems to settle the storms amongst us. "Ethan's been upfront about the situation. We're a team, and we'll handle this together."

His words are meant to bolster, to unite, but the seed of doubt has already been planted. Loyalty is the lifeblood of our sport, a sacred trust that binds us. By merely entertaining the idea of leaving, have I already broken it?

"Team comes first," I finally say, locking eyes with each of my teammates in turn. "Always has."

But even as I speak the creed, the battle within me rages on. I find myself praying for a sign, something to guide me through the fog of indecision.

CHAPTER SIXTEEN: LILY

It's mid-day, and the office buzzes with the kind of organized chaos that only a sports marketing team can truly appreciate. As I review the analytics of our latest social media push, an alert pops up in the corner of the screen. It's a hit on one of the keyword alerts I set up to monitor mentions of the Sabres and any of the players online. Without hesitation, I click on it, expecting the usual mentions, maybe a fan's enthusiastic tweet or a blogger's heated critique.

But this... this is different.

It's a post about a charity event, one that had slipped under my radar. Chicago? Curiosity piqued, I scan the article, skimming past the glossy images and glowing testimonials until a name jumps out at me—Marco "Wild Shot" Silvestri.

What?

According to the post, Marco's been quietly funding scholarships for kids from his old neighborhood in Illinois. I'm taken aback, not just by the revelation but by the disconnect between the man I thought I knew—the party boy who lives for the spotlight—and this secret philanthropist moving in the shadows. "Wild Shot" indeed. He's full of surprises. That same inner-city kid who found solace on frozen ponds is now carving a path for others, offering them escapes of their own.

I click on the hyperlink nestled in the glowing praise, a thread that leads me to a page filled with smiling faces and stories that tug at something deep inside. Each scholarship recipient has penned their gratitude, pouring out tales of dreams that seemed as distant as stars before Marco's generosity pulled them into reach.

"Wow," I murmur under my breath, my eyes scanning the heartfelt testimonials. There's Luis, who talks about becoming the first in his family to attend college, and Maria, whose artistic talents are now being nurtured at a prestigious high school for the arts. They speak of a future made possible by someone I thought I had pegged from the start. My chest tightens, and I feel an unexpected prickle behind my eyelids. The office around me fades into a quiet hum as I'm drawn further into their stories.

I wonder if there are more.

I lean in closer to my computer screen, the soft hum of the office fading to a distant murmur as I click through web page after web page. My fingers fly across the keyboard, tapping out search terms and combing through articles for any scrap of information on Marco's charity work. The more I find, the more my curiosity blooms.

"Anonymous donor pledges substantial sum to local youth center," one headline reads. My heart skips a beat.

The donation dates line up with our home games, times when Marco would be in town, but he never breathed a word of it. I scan through testimonials, pictures of kids with wide, hopeful eyes holding up sports equipment, musical instruments, woodworking supplies—whatever they needed, he provided. It all paints a picture so different from the media's portrayal of him—the relentless party-goer, the playboy forward who leaves defenders and hearts scattered in his wake.

What other secrets does he keep? What drives a man who could have any spotlight to shun it entirely in his most personal endeavors? My chest tightens with a strange cocktail of emotions—admiration, confusion. I push back from my desk, the chair rolling away with a soft squeak that somehow sounds like a sigh. My fingers curl and uncurl as I stand there.

My feet carry me toward the rink almost on their own accord, my eyes tracing the figure eights carved into the ice. It's like he's always there, relentlessly practicing. Marco's form bends and snaps as he executes a perfect slapshot, the puck slamming against the boards with a resounding crack that jolts through me. It's a sound I've come to associate with strength, precision, and now, irony—a tough exterior protecting something unexpectedly tender.

"Nice shot," I say, though the words are just a whisper lost in the cavernous space of the arena.

I need to confront this tangled mess of emotions head-on. No more side-stepping or burying them under piles of work. Marco's secret charity work has thrown me for a loop, making me question not only my judgment of him but also what I truly want.

I pull out my phone, thumb hovering over the screen. It's time to stop observing from the sidelines. I tap out a message to Marco—the man of the hour, the enigma wrapped in a jersey—and hit send before I can second-guess myself.

"Let's talk. Your turf or mine?"

It's bold, maybe too bold, but if today has taught me anything, it's that playing it safe never leads to a win—not in hockey, and certainly not in the complex game of human connections. As I pocket my phone, I feel the stirrings of my nerves.

It's up to him now.

CHAPTER SEVENTEEN: LILY

At home that evening, my phone vibrates against the glass surface of my kitchen table, jolting me from the spreadsheet I've been poring over for the better part of the evening. With a stretch to reach it, I swipe to answer, pressing the device between my shoulder and ear as I continue to scribble down formulas.

"Hey, you've reached Lily, Queen of Hockey Hype—"

"Lily!" The voice on the other end cuts through my playful greeting with the sharpness of a skate blade across ice. It's the last person I ever expected to call me.

"Whoa, Krista. What's got you sounding like you've just missed a penalty shot in overtime?"

"It's bad, Lily," she pants out, and I can practically hear her pacing. "Someone started this awful smear campaign against us. They're all over social media."

"Smear campaign?" I echo, my mind already racing faster than a breakaway. Why wouldn't my alerts catch that? My heart pounds.

"Check the team's accounts. It's a disaster." There's no mistaking the panic lacing her words.

"Okay, I'm on it." I'm all business now. "Just breathe. We'll handle this."

I hang up and leap from my chair. Grabbing my keys, I bolt out of my apartment, the chill of the hallway nipping at my skin, making me wish I'd grabbed a hoodie. But there's no time to waste on regrets or goosebumps; my team needs me.

The drive to the office is a blur of streetlights and the same three thoughts: 'What happened?', 'Who would do this?', and 'How do we fix it?'

When I burst through the doors of the office, the place is as quiet as the stands during a game suspension. I make a beeline for my desk, booting up my computer before my coat is even off. I log into our social media accounts, and my hair falls like a curtain around my face as I lean closer to the screen, as if proximity could somehow shield us from the damage.

There it is. A flood of notifications. Comments, shares, retweets—all spreading vile accusations and fabricated stories like a virus through our fanbase.

Silverpeak Sabres—is Their Newfound Success Serendipity or Steroids?

The original article, posted on a garbage sports tabloid online, is what's started this all. I scroll and scroll, but it's like trying to clear snow from the driveway in a blizzard; it just keeps piling up.

"Great, just what we need," I mutter, my usual humor gone colder than the rink's surface. With every false accusation, I feel a betrayal not just to myself, but to the sport that runs through my veins, taught to me by a father whose own dreams were shattered too soon.

This isn't just a slapshot; this is a full-on body check to our reputation. And I'm going to need more than just my degree to clean up this mess. How do you even begin to dismantle a smear campaign that's spreading faster than gossip in a locker room? My mental playbook is full of tactics for engaging fans and boosting morale, but nothing for when the team's very integrity is body checked into the boards.

"Hey, Morgan." The voice is cool and clipped, slicing through my fog of frustration.

I look up, and there she stands—Krista. Tall, icy-blonde hair sharp as her blue gaze, which studies me like I'm a play she's about to pick apart. It's no secret we clash more than rival teams on the ice; our goals may align, but our methods are worlds apart.

"Krista," I greet cautiously, straightening in my seat. "I told you I would handle this."

She crosses her arms, and I notice, not for the first time, how her posture mimics the confidence of someone who's never had to fight for their spot on the team. "It's bad."

"Understatement of the season," I reply, my instincts bracing for the verbal sparring match that usually follows our exchanges.

"Look, we both want what's best for the team," she states, and it's disarming to hear her speak without that hidden barb. "And right now, the team needs us to put aside our... differences and deal with this."

I study her, searching for the angle because with Krista, there's always an angle. But her face is as unreadable as ever, and I wonder if maybe, just maybe, this crisis has thawed the frost a bit. After all, what's the use of rivalry if there's no team left to fight over?

"Alright," I say slowly. "Let's hear your game plan."

"First," she starts, coming into my office and pulling up a chair—and I can almost see the cogs turning behind those piercing blue eyes, "we draft a clear, concise statement. We lay out the facts, strip away the emotion. It's damage control 101. Test results from every team member."

The suggestion is solid, irritatingly so. I lean back against the cold metal desk in the office—our makeshift war room—and tap a rhythmless beat against its surface.

"Okay, I'm listening," I concede, swallowing the lump of pride in my throat. "What's part two?"

"A press conference," she answers swiftly, as if she's been waiting for me to ask. "We face this head-on, answer questions, show that we have nothing to hide."

I nod, considering the play. It's bold, potentially messy, but it's better than sitting in the penalty box of public opinion. "Alright, let's do it. But remember, this isn't about spinning the story; it's about setting it straight."

Krista's gaze meets mine, and for a fleeting second, I see something other than ambition there – maybe respect, maybe understanding. Or maybe I'm just hoping for an assist where there's only ever been rivalry.

"Understood," she says, and there's a trace of warmth there that makes me think this temporary truce could turn the tide of the game.

"Good," I reply, standing up. "Let's call the guys."

***

Hours later, it's just me and Krista, surrounded by crumpled paper drafts and half-empty coffee cups. It's late, the kind of late that blurs the lines between 'dedicated' and 'delusional', but quitting isn't in my playbook. We got every on-roster player scheduled for a drug test bright and early, and if we keep going like this, Krista and I will both still be awake. The clinic has even agreed to process the tests within the hour for us.

"Try this," I suggest, reading over the latest version of our statement. "We are committed to maintaining an environment of integrity and respect, both on and off the ice." I feel the weight of each word, heavy with truth and the promise of what our team stands for.

Krista leans over, her icy eyes scanning the sentence as she nods. "It's good. It's us." For once, there's no edge to her voice, no sharp jabs or hidden agendas—just teamwork, raw and real.

Morning comes too soon, dressed in the gray light of dawn and the buzz of anticipation. The press conference room is filled with the scent of polished wood and the low murmur of reporters gathering like vultures. After a mad dash to our respective apartments to get presentable, Krista and I stand side by side at the podium, an unexpected duo to anyone who knows the friction between us.

"Thank you for joining us today," I begin, my voice steady despite the butterflies playing hockey in my stomach. "We'd like to address the recent claims made against our hockey team."

"As many of you are aware," Krista takes over, her tone confident and controlled, "there have been several allegations circulating on social media platforms regarding substance use by our players."

I step in, offering the evidence we've prepared—clean test results for each and every player—that tell a story far different from the one painted by our anonymous critics. "These documents clearly show that not only are the accusations unfounded, but they're maliciously fabricated."

The room is silent, every reporter scribbling notes or holding up recorders like shields. I can almost hear the collective breath being held, waiting for us to stumble, to give them the slip-up they crave.

But we don't falter. We stand united, two women who've spent more time at each other's throats than on the same side, fighting for something bigger than ourselves. And as I look over at Krista, her blonde hair like a halo under the bright lights, I realize that maybe, just maybe, there's more to her than the ambition I've always resented.

"Any questions?" Krista asks, and the vultures swoop in with talons bared, ready to tear apart our defense. But we're ready for them, armed with the truth and an unspoken pact to protect our team, our family, at any cost.

I'm standing there, heart hammering in my chest as the last question hangs in the air, almost tangible in its weight. Krista's cool gaze sweeps over the sea of reporters before she answers with a precision that slices through the tension. The crowd is visibly swayed; I can see it in the way their skeptical frowns soften and the furrowed brows relax.

"Thank you for your attention to this matter," I add, my voice steady despite the adrenaline rush. "We believe in the integrity of our team and are glad to have had the opportunity to clarify these issues."

After the press conference concludes, the buzz doesn't die down—it shifts from frenzied speculation to murmurs of impressed acknowledgment. Even Thompson, our usually stoic coach, has a glimmer of approval in his eyes as he nods at us both, a rare display of emotion that speaks volumes.

"Good job out there," he says gruffly, and I feel a smile tugging at my lips.

"Thanks, Thompson," Krista replies smoothly, and I catch her eye for a split second, acknowledging the moment.

As we step outside, I pull my phone from my pocket, scrolling quickly through notifications. Tweets, comments, articles—all painting us in a new light, a victorious hue that contrasts starkly with the dark cloud of allegations that loomed over us mere hours ago.

"Looks like we might actually have turned the tide," I muse aloud, my eyes flickering up to Krista, who stands beside me, her posture relaxed but her eyes sharp, scanning the headlines on her own device.

"Never doubted it for a second," she says, but there's an uncharacteristic warmth in her tone that catches me off guard.

"Krista, I—" I start, the words catching in my throat. I'm not one for sentimentality, especially not with her, but the gratitude bubbling inside me feels too big to contain. "Thank you. For all of this. I didn't expect you to step up like you did."

She gives me a sidelong glance, her expression unreadable. Then, she turns to me. “I leaked that photo of you and Marco.”

My mouth practically drops. “What? Why?”

She sighs and rolls her eyes. I notice that she didn’t apologize—only confessed. “I wanted you out of here. But, now…I see what you can do. You’ve got some substance. And you can help the team. So, for now, we're on the same team, Lily. Whatever it takes to win, right?"

"Right," I echo, though her words leave me with more questions than answers. The uneasy feeling creeps back in, the one that suggests there's a layer to Krista I haven't peeled back yet. Is helping me just another strategic move in her game? Another rung on her ladder?

"Controversy or not, if there's no team, there's no way for me to get ahead." She crosses her arms. "And I didn't claw my way up here to lose footing over some baseless rumors against the whole of the Sabres."

Her words hang in the air, coated in that typical Krista frost. All at once, it’s clear – our brief alliance was nothing more than a ceasefire. And now, the rivalry is back with a vengeance.

"Then let's ensure it doesn't happen again," I say, feeling the competitive edge sharpening my own resolve. "We've got to be on top of our game, Krista. Both of us."

"Always am," she fires back with a smirk.

Despite the crackling tension between us, a part of me recognizes the value of this uneasy partnership. We're like opposing players forced onto the same line, each with our own style, but with one goal in mind. It's true, I don't trust her, but there's no denying that two heads are better than one, especially when they're as cunning as Krista's.

"You did nice work today," she murmurs without looking up, but there's a sincerity there that wasn't present yesterday.

"Thanks," I reply, my voice cautious. "You too." Then, I blurt, "Didn't know you had it in you to play nice."

"Only when absolutely necessary," she says, a wisp of her usual frost returning. She finally looks up, locking gazes with me. "For the team, right?"

"Right." The word tastes strange on my tongue, not bitter, not sweet. Just... unexpected.

As the quiet settles between us, I find myself reflecting on this alliance that has formed between Krista and me. Appreciation for her help tonight bubbles inside me, a strange sensation given our history of rivalry.

"See you tomorrow, Morgan," Krista says.

"Tomorrow," I echo, gathering my things.

Walking away from the arena, I know that, as the seasons change, so too could the dynamics of our truce. But I'm not naive enough to think Krista's motives are purely altruistic. No, she's as strategic off the ice as any player is on it — probably more so. While I know I owe part of tonight's victory to her, my gut tells me to be wary, to keep my guard up.

I'm exhausted, and my mind is whirling. But a thought strikes me as soon as I make it home and toss my keys onto the counter—Marco hasn't replied to my text. I didn't see him this morning in the flurry of activity. Krista was the one who'd reached out to get the guys to their testing lab.

It hits me—he's avoiding me.

Even as tired as I am, I grab my keys again.

I know where he goes every morning.

CHAPTER EIGHTEEN: MARCO

The scent of sweat and ice fills my nostrils as I lace up my skates, the sound echoing off the locker room walls. The quiet is a sanctuary before the chaos of practice, where I can let the rhythm of wrapping tape around my stick be a kind of meditation. It's just me and the hum of the overhead lights until the door swings open with more force than necessary.

I don't need to look up to know it's Lily; the purpose in her stride is unmistakable. Her those sharp eyes of hers are fixed on me, and she moves with a confidence that's all her own.

"Marco Silvestri," she says, planting herself in front of my locker, hands on hips, "we need to talk."

I keep my focus on the curve of my stick blade, feigning indifference. "If this is about the new promo campaign, can it wait? Practice is about to start."

She shakes her head, brushing off my attempt to sidestep her like an amateur defender. "No, this isn't about some marketing strategy. This is about you playing secret Santa with college funds."

My hands still for a moment, and I reluctantly meet her gaze. "What are you talking about?"

"Cut the crap, Wild Shot." Her use of my nickname lacks its usual playful lilt. "I've done my digging. Those anonymous scholarships funded by *you*."

I try to maintain a casual shrug, but there's an edge of tension creeping into my muscles. "So what if they are? Last I checked, giving away money wasn't a crime."

"Then why keep it a secret?" Lily's voice holds a note of challenge, but beneath it, I can hear something else—curiosity, maybe even admiration.

"Maybe I don't want the attention," I say, standing up now, towering over her slightly. But Lily Morgan doesn't back down—not from me, not from anyone.

"Or maybe," she pushes, "there's more to Marco Silvestri than late-night parties and highlight-reel goals."

I let out a breath, feeling the walls I've built around myself wobbling under her scrutiny. Lily has a way of doing that, of making you want to be more than the sum of your stats and your reputation. It's one of the things that irks me—and pulls me—in equal measure. But I've already confide din her—and she pulled away. Why is she pushing now?

"Look," I finally relent, "it's personal, okay? Can we leave it at that?"

"Personal how?" Now she steps closer, her intensity dialing up another notch. "You owe me an explanation, Marco. If you're part of this team, if you're part of what I'm trying to build here, then I need to know where your head's at."

And damn it if she isn't right. Because despite every instinct telling me to keep my guard up, to play the carefree jock everyone expects me to be, Lily's belief in something greater makes me want to drop the act—if only for a moment.

"Look, Lily..." My voice trails off, and I shuffle uncomfortably, suddenly conscious of the weight of my stick in my hands. "You don't get it. This—hockey, the scholarships—it's complicated."

"Then uncomplicate it for me," she insists, tilting her head, waiting for me to continue.

"Can we not do this here?" I ask. Her persistence is admirable, but the vulnerability she's unwittingly coaxing out of me feels foreign, unwelcome. And I don't trust her not to go cold again.

Lily nods, her eyes softening just enough to remind me that beneath the marketer and the strategist, there's a woman who cares deeply—about hockey, about the team, and maybe, just maybe, about the guy who's spent far too long hiding behind a facade.

"Okay, after practice," she agrees, and then, with a curt nod that feels like a temporary truce, she turns on her heel and leaves me to my thoughts, which are now anything but quiet.

The ice calls to me, a siren song that's always been my refuge. I skate out for practice with the same nonchalance I've honed to an art form, pushing Lily's confrontation—and my recent angst over the cooling-off of our *situationship*—to the back of my mind.

I can feel her watching me as I join the flow of the practice, pucks clattering against the boards, sticks clashing. The familiar sounds ground me, but Lily's presence at the edge of the rink is a new variable, an unexpected audience. She's not just any spectator, though. She's Lily Morgan, the woman who managed to find a chink in Marco Silvestri's well-armored exterior. The same woman who will sit across from me later, expecting more truths that I've never shared with anyone else.

For now, though, I focus on the puck, on the ice, on the game that both shields and defines me. Later, with Lily, I'll face whatever comes. But until then, I'll be the untouchable Marco Silvestri, one stride ahead of everyone else, including my own demons.

***

Practice lasts too long but is over too soon.

The chill of the locker room can't compete with the cold knot of nerves in my stomach as I unlatch my helmet and drop it on the bench. My fingers are unsteady, betraying a vulnerability I'm not used to feeling, let alone showing. I waited until everyone else was gone, doing laps on the rink by myself, a punishing pace that has left my legs burning as much as my conflicted heart. But I couldn't avoid it forever. So now, here I am.

"Tell me about the scholarships." Lily's voice echoes off the cinderblock walls, and she's standing there with that same determination I noticed earlier, like she's ready to skate into battle.

My chest tightens. This isn't just about money or philanthropy; it's about my past – a past I've kept buried beneath layers of swagger and arrogance.

"It's... complicated."

"Complicated how?" She steps closer. Her green eyes aren't just looking at me; they're searching me, demanding the truth I've hidden from everyone else.

"Look, I grew up in a place where dreams were luxury items. And sometimes, so was food, electricity, new shoes. I had to do a lot to help take care of my family, young. I was angry about a lot of things when I was younger. Hockey... it was my way out, you know?" I begin, tracing a scar on my forearm absently. "I was recruited out of high school, but not everyone gets out. So, I give back. It's like trying to settle a score with a past that never really leaves you."

Lily's gaze softens as she listens, her stance relaxing a fraction. I can see her processing my confession, the pieces clicking together behind those sharp eyes.

"Marco..." Her voice is gentler now, less about confrontation and more about understanding. "That's incredible. Why keep it a secret?"

"Because," I say, my throat tightening, "it's not about recognition. It's about doing something right in a life that started wrong. It's about redemption, Lily. Maybe if I can help someone else find their way, it means I'm not completely lost myself."

She nods slowly, absorbing every word.

"Thank you for telling me," she says softly. "I had no idea."

"Nobody does," I reply, but the usual satisfaction in keeping my secrets doesn't come. Instead, there's relief, a weight lifting that I didn't realize I'd been carrying until now.

I rake a hand through my hair, the damp strands clinging to my fingers. The air in the locker room is heavy, laced with the musk of exertion and the sharp tang of disinfectant

"Marco, I..." She hesitates.

"Spit it out, Morgan," I say, though my tone lacks its usual bite. I'm raw, nerves exposed, and if she's going to take a shot at me, I'd rather she just get on with it.

She steps closer. "Until the night you told me about your dad, I never saw this side of you. You always seemed so—"

"Carefree? Self-absorbed?" I supply the words, half mocking.

"Confident," she corrects softly. "But now, seeing this vulnerability... I realize there's so much more to you."

My chest tightens, and I swallow hard. "Lily, I—" I cut myself off, the intensity of what I feel threatening to choke me.

"Tell me," she encourages, her voice a whisper meant only for me.

"Ever since we started this...pretend relationship," I begin, watching her reaction closely, "I've found myself caught up in it. More than I should be." My gaze locks onto hers, willing her to understand. "It was supposed to be just for show, you know? Easy. Fun."

"And?" She prompts, her hand inching toward mine as if drawn by a magnetic force.

"And I enjoy every second with you," I admit, my voice dropping to a husky timbre. "Every laugh, every glare when I push your buttons. It's all real for me, Lily. I didn't expect to feel this way, but I do. And when I told you about my dad, and you went cold on me—damn. It hurt. A lot."

There it is. The truth laid bare between us.

Lily blinks, her lips parting slightly as if she's about to speak, but no words come out. I can see her mind racing behind those sharp eyes, trying to make sense of my confession, trying to gauge the sincerity in my expression.

"Marco—" She starts but stops herself, her breath catching. There's a tremor in her voice that matches the one in my hands. We're both unsteady.

"Look, I don't expect anything from you, Lily. I just wanted you to know," I say quickly, the fear of rejection creeping in, icing over the warmth that had begun to thaw my guarded heart.

She takes a deep breath, steadying herself, and I brace for impact. But instead of words, she gives me a small, uncertain smile—a flicker of something genuine and warm that fans the embers of hope in my chest.

"I think I've been so focused on the game plan that I didn't see...this." Her words hang in the air, and she gestures vaguely between us, her eyes searching mine for something I'm not sure I can give.

"See what, Lily?" I find myself drawn to her, each step closing the distance until the warmth of her seems to envelop me, drawing me in like the promise of victory after a hard-fought game.

"This," she whispers, her voice barely audible over the pounding of my heart, which seems to recognize the significance of this moment even before my mind can catch up.

And then, without another thought, I bridge the gap between us. My lips meet hers with a urgency that surprises even me, fueled by all the passion and intensity that's been simmering beneath the surface of every glance, every touch, every word we've exchanged. It's more than just a kiss; it's a clash of everything we are, everything we've been holding back. It's reckless, it's sweet, it's a declaration made without words.

In this moment, everything else falls away—the competition, the pressures, the expectations. All that exists is the raw, unfiltered connection between us, the undeniable electricity that's been building to this crescendo. From my perspective, the moment our lips touch, the world shifts. There's an intensity in her response that catches me off guard, her hands gripping my jersey as if to pull me even closer, to erase any space that remains between us. The connection ignites something fierce and undeniable, a blaze that consumes all doubt, all hesitation.

When we finally part, gasping for air, the world comes rushing back, but it's changed somehow. I see her—Lily, the woman who's shattered every barrier I've put up around myself.

And then, pulling away, I grab my shower bag and towel from my locker. My head is spinning. Without another word, I leave her standing there, open-mouthed, looking shellshocked.

I have no idea what I've just done—but this time, I run away.

CHAPTER NINETEEN: ETHAN

The letter feels heavier than it should, the crisp paper in my grasp a tangible symbol of opportunity—and a potential goodbye. I'm alone in my apartment, the quiet hum of the refrigerator the only sound accompanying my brooding. My eyes flick over the words "transfer offer" again, and my mind starts to churn with what this means for me, Ethan Scott, defenseman with dreams bigger than the rink I've called home for years.

I lean back in my chair, rolling the tension from my shoulders. This could be it, the big break. Better team, better exposure. My heartbeat picks up at the thought of playing alongside some of the greats, my name chanted by a crowd that's twice as large, my face on billboards and in commercials. The sponsors are no joke either—signing deals that could set me up comfortably and ease any financial worry for my family.

But then there's the flip side. I press my thumb against the embossed seal of the letter, feeling its ridges. Playing for a better team also means fiercer competition for my position. The comfort of knowing my teammates' plays, their strengths and weaknesses—all of it would be gone. I'd be the new guy, having to prove myself all over again.

"Is it worth it?" I mutter to the empty room, my voice sounding oddly foreign in the silence. I've always been a team player, molded by the values of camaraderie and loyalty. A new team wouldn't just be a new jersey; it would mean leaving behind a brotherhood.

I stand up, pacing the length of my small living room, the offer letter now a crumpled mess in my fist. The possibility of furthering my career is tempting, almost intoxicating. But the question remains: At what cost?

This isn't just about hockey. It's about where I want my life to go. And sure, this offer looks shiny and promising on paper, but what's a career without people to share the victories with, without a community that feels like home?

I come to a stop in front of the window, gazing down at the street below, where life moves with an oblivious hustle. I've got a decision to make, and it's not just about where I play—it's about who I want to be, both on the ice and off it.

"Damn it." I run a hand through my hair, a familiar restlessness settling in my chest. The pros and cons list in my head is dead even, each argument met with a counterpoint just as strong.

In this restless dance, my thoughts keep circling back to Lily – Lily, who breezed into our team like a fresh gust of northern wind, altering the landscape of our little hockey community with the force of her presence. Since her arrival, the stands have been spilling over with fans, their cheers louder, their spirits higher. It's like she's injected life into every corner of the arena, and by extension, the entire team.

She's a whirlwind of action – setting up community service projects where we'd help refurbish rundown parts of the community or spend Saturdays teaching kids to skate for free. She's even convinced a bunch of local businesses to sponsor these events. Now, the local storefronts proudly display our team's merch alongside their own, a tangible sign of unity and mutual support.

With a sigh, I drop into the couch, the leather cool against my skin. The answer isn't in the letter; it never was.

"Dammit, Lily," I say, the words a half-laugh, half-groan as I lean my head against the couch. "You're making this so hard."

Because it's more than just admiration now, isn't it? There's a warmth that spreads through my chest whenever I catch sight of her across the ice, a twist in my gut when I overhear her bantering with Marco. And speaking of Marco—Wild Shot Silvestri, with his easy charm and relentless flirtation. He's got her smiling in ways that I never could, and that stings more than any body check ever could.

"Could have been me," I whisper to the empty room, my voice thick with a regret that's as sharp as a skate blade. There were moments, fleeting seconds when I thought maybe, just maybe, she was looking at me with something more in those green eyes. Moments I let slip through my fingers.

Could still be you, a rebellious part of my mind suggests, but it's quickly silenced by the image of her and Marco laughing together, their chemistry undeniable. The missed opportunities stack up like pucks in a practice drill, each one a shot I didn't take.

The thought of leaving now, with Lily transforming this team from the inside out, gnaws at me. She's become the heartbeat of this place. My dreams have always been clear-cut paths down the ice, but she's etched new lines, complicating the play with every smile that doesn't quite meet her eyes when she looks at Marco. I hate admitting even to myself that I'm afraid—afraid of losing what might never have been mine to begin with.

I cross the room to my desk, pulling open the drawer where memories and mementos are kept—the ticket stubs, the worn-out gloves, the snapshots of victories and losses. There's a sanctity here, a collection of moments that define me not just as a player but as a man.

The letter slips into the drawer, lying dormant amongst the relics of my past. As I push it closed, there's a sense of closure too, a chapter ending so a new one can begin.

And who knows? Maybe one day, the lines between friendship and something more will blur with Lily. But for now, I'm committed to the present. That's enough. It has to be.

And with that, I head out the door, decision made, ready to face whatever comes next.

I know, deep down, I've made the right call.

CHAPTER TWENTY: LILY

The persistent buzz of my phone drags me out of sleep, an incessant vibration that promises nothing good. I groan, the sound muffled by the pillow half-smothering my face, and fumble blindly on the nightstand for the offending device.

"Come on," I mutter to myself, my fingers finally closing around the cool, sleek edges of my phone. With a resigned sigh, I lift my head, crack one eye open, and squint at the glowing screen.

Holy slap shot... The notifications are relentless, flashing like warning lights on the dashboard of my suddenly spiraling day. I have flashbacks to the false doping scandal as I sit up, trying to rub the sleep from my vision while scrolling through the endless alerts.

"Great, just great," I grumble, my voice thick with sleep and frustration.

Each ping is another mention, another comment, another share of a photo—me and Marco, kissing in the locker room. Caught in a moment meant to be private, now splashed across social media.

Who could have done this?

I swipe through the messages. It's not just fans and nosy netizens; it's friends, family, and worse, the hawk-eyed hockey community that can make or break you.

"Marco's going to flip his lid..." I whisper, picturing his deep brown eyes clouded with the same mix of shock and anger that's brewing in mine. We're in this mess together, whether we like it or not.

I toss back the covers and swing my legs over the side of the bed, the chill of the morning nipping at my bare skin. This isn't how I planned to start my day.

My fingers fumble for a moment before finding his contact, and I hit call, heart drumming a frantic rhythm against my ribs.

"Hello?" His voice, usually so full of cocky confidence, now holds a thread of tension that mirrors my own.

"Marco, have you seen—" My voice breaks, a tremor betraying the worry knotted tight in my chest.

"Yeah, I've seen it." He cuts me off, his deep voice rough around the edges. "We need to meet. Now."

"Agreed." I swallow hard, fighting back the swell of emotions. There's a pause, a silent acknowledgement of the storm we're about to weather together.

"Let's grab a coffee and figure this out." His attempt at casualness doesn't quite mask the urgency.

"Okay, see you soon." I hang up, battling the blend of anger and vulnerability coursing through me.

The chill of damage-control mode replaces the heat of panic as I yank open my closet door. My fingers dance along the hangers, skimming past jerseys and comfortable tees until they snag on the fabric that feels just right—the blend of casual and professional that this disaster demands. A navy blazer that's structured but not stuffy, a white v-neck tee that's soft but not slouchy, and a pair of dark jeans that scream 'I mean business' without actually having to say it. It's an ensemble that nods to a no-nonsense approach to crises.

I step into a pair of ankle boots with enough heel to elevate my posture yet grounded enough to run the metaphorical rink if need be. With a glance in the mirror, I rake my fingers through my hair, giving it a semblance of order. Makeup is minimal—just a touch to ward off the ghostly pallor of shock. My green eyes stare back at me, fierce.

I grab my phone, keys, and the confidence that has always been my best accessory.

The coffee shop is a quiet haven compared to the deafening roar of speculation and judgment waiting outside its doors. Marco's there, and even from the entrance, I can see the storm clouds gathering in his deep brown eyes.

"Wild Shot" Silvestri, always the life of the party, now looks like he's been sucker-punched by life itself. As I approach, I notice his hands clasped around a mug—white-knuckled.

"Hey," I greet him, voice steadier than I feel. He glances up, and the edges of his frustration soften slightly.

"Hey, Lily." His use of my name is a reminder that despite the new scandal, some things remain unchanged.

We exchange a look that says more than words ever could—we're in this together, come hell or high water. And as I slide into the seat across from him, I know this isn't just about damage control anymore. It's about us, our reputations, and the uncharted ice we're about to tread.

"First things first," I start, voice low, "we need to get ahead of the narrative. Control the story before it controls us." My words are clipped, professional, but inside, a storm of uncertainty rages. My fingers hover over the screen of my phone, the digital keyboard a battlefield where each letter is a potential ally or foe. Marco watches, his espresso untouched as it releases spirals of steam into the air between us — a foggy curtain drawn around our crisis.

"We should open with... 'To our fans and community'—because that's who we're really talking to here."

"Right," Marco nods. "We acknowledge them first. Show we care about their perspective."

I type swiftly, crafting our opening line, feeling the weight of every word. This isn't just about damage control; it's about shaping the narrative, taking the reins back from whoever dared to loosen them from our grasp. My thumbs dance across my phone, tapping out our joint statement, our united front.

"Here's what I've got so far." I clear my throat, reading aloud to give the words life, to test their strength. "'To our fans and community, we want to address the photo circulating online.'" I pause, waiting for his nod to continue. "'What was shared was a private moment, never intended for public consumption.'"

"Good. It's direct, apologetic without being overly defensive," he says, his analytical mind dissecting our strategy as if we're planning a game-winning play.

"Should we say something about our relationship? Clarify things?" The question hangs in the air like a puck suspended mid-shot.

"Maybe just a touch on professionalism," he suggests, his eyes locking onto mine with an intensity that's both unnerving and reassuring. "Remind them that we're here for hockey, first and foremost."

"Agreed." I add another sentence, the clacking of keys punctuating our resolve. "'Our commitment to the team and the sport remains, and this incident does not reflect the professional nature of our relationship while we are on campus.'"

"Put in something about respecting privacy, too," he adds, shifting uncomfortably. "This isn't just about us. It's about setting boundaries."

"Of course." And so I weave in our plea, a call for understanding in a world that often forgets the humanity behind the headlines. "'We kindly ask for your respect and understanding as we navigate this personal matter.'"

"Sounds good, Lily," Marco concedes, offering a small, appreciative smile. "It's honest, straightforward."

"Thanks." I exhale, scanning the draft one last time before looking up at him. "Ready to hit send?"

He reaches across the table, placing his hand over mine. "Together," he says, and there's a promise in that one word, a pact sealed not by signatures but by vulnerability.

"Alright, together," I echo, and with a collective breath held between us, my thumb presses down, sending our crafted truth out into the world.

"Sent," I announce, unable to keep my voice from wavering just a fraction.

Marco, sitting across from me, runs a hand through his dark hair—a nervous gesture that belies his usual cool demeanor. "And now we wait."

It's barely a heartbeat before my phone vibrates with incoming messages. Krista's response is as swift as it is predictable, her words displayed in a neat, icy font on the screen: "Saw the draft. Good luck controlling this wildfire. You'll need it."

"Does she ever not sound like she's perched on a throne of daggers?" I mutter under my breath, locking my phone before I'm tempted to fire off a retort.

"Krista being Krista," Marco says with a dismissive shrug, but his eyes are hard, a storm brewing in their depths. "What about Thompson?"

"Concerned, mostly." I paraphrase our coach's message from my drive over from memory. "'We'll get through this, but stick to hockey and stay out of the tabloids.' He's not wrong."

"Right." Marco exhales, frustration etching lines across his forehead. "This—us—it's not just locker room talk anymore. It's out there, and we have to deal with it."

"Deal with it," I echo, the words tasting bitter.

He leans forward, his elbows resting on the table, the intensity back in his gaze. "Lily, no scandal can change how I feel about the game. Or about—"

"Us?" I supply when he hesitates, my heart thudding against my ribs.

"Us," he confirms with a nod. "We can't let it break us."

My phones dings again, and then again. And then, I have to silence the notifications. We watch as comments flood in beneath our joint statement—a stream of judgement where every word, emoji, and like is a decree on our fate.

"Look at this one," Marco says, pointing to a particularly supportive message that stands out amongst the sea of disappointment and outrage. "'Everybody deserves a moment of privacy. Hang in there!' At least some people get it."

I lean in closer, squinting at the tiny font. A warmth spreads through me, ignited by an anonymous username's compassion. But for every positive comment, there's a wave of negative ones ready to extinguish it.

"Here comes the bad stuff," I murmur, scrolling past a particularly vicious string of exclamation points and harsh words. "We're 'disgraceful,' apparently. Sullying a professional environment to use the college as our personal playground."

Marco snorts, a wry twist to his lips. "They act like they've never had a moment they wouldn't want plastered all over the internet."

"Except ours really *is* all over the internet," I shoot back, unable to suppress the bitterness creeping into my voice. This was supposed to be damage control, but all I feel is more exposed, more vulnerable. I wince at a new comment, holding my phone out to Marco.

"Is this what my tuition is paying for? Get your own room. Ouch."

"Let's focus on what we can control," Marco insists, pulling me back to the present. "We stick by the story, keep things professional, and let the hockey speak for itself."

"Speaking of which, there's a game tomorrow," I add, trying to latch onto something solid—the ice, the players, the sound of a puck against a stick. Things I understand, things I can influence without fear of them spiraling out of control.

"Exactly," he nods vigorously. "We show them that the team's stronger than ever, and this..." He gestures vaguely to the phone between us, "...is just a blip."

"Right. A blip." I repeat the word, focusing on its insignificance. A blip is small, manageable. We can handle a blip.

The fans, the media, the entire league can come at us with their scrutiny and their judgement. But they don't know us—not really. They don't know how fiercely I protect my team, or how Marco can turn any situation around.

Stepping out of the coffee shop, the door swings shut behind us with a muted jangle. The city's hustle bleeds into my awareness. My boots click in rhythm on the sidewalk, echoing the pounding of my heart as I glance over at Marco.

"Man, it's chilly," he mutters, drawing his jacket tighter around him. His breath puffs out in visible clouds, each one dissipating quickly, much like our attempts to contain the fallout. We're two figures caught in a still frame, a snapshot before the storm really hits.

"Feels like a sign," I say, trying to inject some humor into the heaviness that hangs between us. "Even the weather's giving us the cold shoulder."

Marco's lips twitch, not quite making it to a full smile, but it's enough to remind me of the mischievous spark that usually dances in his deep brown eyes. "You know what they say, Lil. If you can't take the heat..."

"Get out of the locker room?" I finish for him, feeling the corner of my mouth lift despite the unease knotting my stomach.

"Exactly." He shoves his hands into his pockets, shoulders squared against more than just the cold. I appreciate the effort; we're both playing roles now—the indomitable duo.

We walk in sync, side by side, battling the same invisible adversary. With each step, I feel a little piece of my earlier panic shed away, replaced by something sturdier—stubbornness. It's there, a shield being forged with every footfall.

As we reach the corner, the traffic light blinks to red, urging us to halt. The intersection feels symbolic, a pause in the path ahead, filled with choices and consequences. I draw in a breath, letting the crisp air fill my lungs, bracing for what's to come.

The light flips to green, and together, we step off the curb. There's no going back, only forward—through the scrutiny, the judgement, the whispers and stares. But we're moving in unison, a united front ready to face whatever play comes our way. We have playoffs tonight, and I won't let this side noise derail us.

But after the game, no matter the outcome, I have made another choice—and I'm going to admit my feelings tonight.

CHAPTER TWENTY ONE: LILY

The roar of the crowd echoes in my ears, a thunderous applause that marks the culmination of another grueling season. One playoff game down. I’m overjoyed as I navigate the labyrinthine corridors beneath the arena. The scent of sweat and victory lingers heavily in the air, reminding me of the battle fought on the ice tonight.

I'm not just here to congratulate the team; I have a mission. My heart pounds against my ribcage like it's trying to escape, each beat syncing with my purposeful strides. As I reach the entrance to the locker room, my hand hesitates on the door handle, but only for a moment. I can't afford doubt now, not when everything I feel is at stake.

"Here goes nothing," I mutter to myself and push the door open.

The cacophony of celebration hits me immediately—laughter, cheers, the clinking of bottles. Amidst the sea of jerseys, he stands out: Marco, his dark hair tousled and damp with exertion, his olive skin glowing under the fluorescent lights. His deep brown eyes find mine, and that mischievous smirk that's infuriatingly charming spreads across his face.

"Hey there, Lily," he says, his voice a warm melody over the noise. He's basking in the glory of the win, and why shouldn't he? Tonight, he scored the goal that clinched our victory. But I'm not here to talk about hockey. Not this time.

"Marco," I reply, my own voice steady despite the storm of nerves inside me. I take a step closer, my eyes locked on his, determined to bridge the gap between us with more than just words. The room seems to fade around us, the celebrations dulling into the background as we stand in our own little pocket of reality.

"Can you believe this? We did it, Lils!" he exclaims, oblivious to the internal struggle that's been eating away at me for weeks now. The sound of his nickname for me sends a shiver down my spine, a reminder of how close we've become and yet how much I've kept hidden.

"Marco," I say, and it's like I'm hearing my own voice for the first time—clear, resolute. "I need to talk to you about something important."

For a moment, his smile is unchanging, that trademark grin of the hotshot forward who thrives in the limelight. Then it wavers, his face registering a shift as he reads something in my eyes—a gravity he's not used to seeing from me. The smile doesn't disappear entirely, but it shrinks, replaced by a more measured expression, one that's open and attentive.

"Sure, Lily," Marco replies, his tone dropping to match mine. He steps away from the others, signaling a boundary between their revelry and our sudden island of solemnity. All at once, the aura of 'Wild Shot' Silvestri, the scorer of tonight's winning goal, fades into the background, giving way to just Marco—my teammate, and possibly something more.

"Everything okay?" he asks, his deep brown eyes searching mine for clues.

As he looks at me, really looks, it's clear he's putting aside his natural inclination for mischief, ready to listen. And for a brief second, I allow myself to marvel at this side of him that so few get to witness—the thoughtful man beneath the charming rogue. It's this glimpse of sincerity that reminds me why I'm standing here in the first place, why my heart won't stop pounding its rhythm against my ribcage.

Steeling myself, I break the silence that has fallen between us. "Marco, I've been carrying around these feelings, and it's time I let them loose."

His eyebrows arch, but he doesn't interrupt. The familiar scent of the locker room—rubber, sweat—fills my nostrils, grounding me.

"Look, I can't keep pretending it's nothing," I continue, my voice betraying the rush of emotions I've been checking at the boards for too long. "I like you, Marco. A lot. And it's been driving me crazy because there's also Ethan—"

His reaction is immediate, his features registering shock, but only for an instant. Then, as if he's just received the puck on his stick and is calculating his next move, his expression shifts. His eyes, those deep pools of brown that have teased and taunted me from across the ice and in the corridors of the arena, now draw me in with a gentleness I hadn't seen before.

"Wow, Lily," Marco breathes out, his voice quieter than I've ever heard it. He runs a hand through his dark, tousled hair, a sign that I've thrown him off his game. But he doesn't look away, doesn't back down. Instead, he steps into this unexpected play like the pro he is. "I wasn't expecting the part about Ethan."

He's listening intently now, his usual bravado stripped clean, leaving behind a raw openness that speaks volumes.

"Please, go on," he urges softly, giving me the space to lay it all out on the line.

My fingers are ice-cold as they clutch at the hem of my jacket. Marco's proximity is a magnetic field, pulling me closer despite the tempest of emotions swirling inside me.

"Marco," I start, my voice barely above a whisper, "I need to know... do you feel anything for me?" The words hang heavy in the air. "I know what you said in the locker room before you kissed me. But I have to be sure…"

There's a pause, and for a moment, the only sounds are the distant echoes of celebration. Then, he moves—a simple step that bridges the gap between us. The locker room suddenly feels too small, the walls reverberating with the thunderous beat of my heart.

"Lily," Marco says, his voice laced with an earnestness that slices through the tension. His gaze holds mine captive. "I've fallen for you too."

The admission hangs between us, potent and electrifying. In his eyes, I see the reflection of my own tangled feelings—the mix of excitement and love, and something deeper, more vulnerable.

And just like that, we're no longer just Lily and Marco, the marketing whiz and the hotshot forward. We're two people standing on the precipice of something terrifyingly real, something neither of us anticipated but somehow always felt inevitable.

Relief crashes into me, and I'm certain my knees would give out if not for Marco. I reach for his hand, my fingers sliding against his. His palm is rough, calloused from years on the rink, but his touch is tender.

"Marco," I start, my voice steady despite the whirlwind inside me. "I can't believe—"

"Hey," he cuts in, a shadow of his usual mischievous grin playing on his lips. "You don't have to say anything else." He squeezes my hand, grounding me. "I want this, Lily. You and me."

But just as quickly as his smile appears, it's replaced by a contemplative frown, the kind that usually precedes a well-thought-out play. "We should keep it low-key, though. At least until the playoffs wrap up." His eyes search mine, seeking understanding. "No distractions, right? We both need to focus."

I nod, not because I love the idea of hiding, but because I get it. Hockey is more than a game—it's a commitment, and neither of us can afford to lose sight of our goals. Not when we've worked so hard to get here. Not when we've been plagued by roadblock after roadblock.

"And please know that I desperately want to kiss you right now, but I'm crazy paranoid after that picture got leaked—so just imagine getting seriously kissed right now. Very seriously."

"Okay," I agree, feeling both a heat rise into my cheeks and a twinge in my chest at the thought of any more secret stolen moments. Neither of us want that—the invasion of privacy, not the kiss. I definitely want that. But he's right. "For now, it'll be our little hat trick."

"Perfect." He flashes a grin, all confidence and warmth, and for a second, I forget about the secrecy, the complications, the what-ifs. There's just the two of us, united by something that feels a lot like team spirit—but for the heart.

"Think we can pull this off without the team catching on?" I ask.

Marco's chuckle is low and confident, a sound that sends a shiver of anticipation down my spine. "Lily, I've been dodging defensemen since I was six. Keeping a secret? That's rookie stuff."

But it's more than just a secret; it's us, Marco and me, against the world—or at least against the prying eyes of the hockey community. The thought both terrifies and electrifies me.

"Besides," he continues, his thumb tracing circles on the back of my hand, "Playoffs will be a cinch. We've got an advantage. You know this game inside out, not just the plays, but the heart of it. And you've got me, Wild Shot Silvestri, who never misses a goal—or so they say."

I roll my eyes but smile. His arrogance is part of his charm, a layer of bravado covering up the thoughtful guy underneath. The one who's seen struggles I'm only beginning to understand.

"Never misses a goal, huh?" I tease. "Guess I really scored then, if you're head over blades for me."

"Scored big time," he agrees, leaning in so close I can feel the warmth of his breath against my cheek. I feel a little dizzy.

This is going to be a *lot* harder secret to keep than I thought.

CHAPTER TWENTY TWO: ETHAN

Ice clings to my blades like a second skin, the chill of the rink a familiar comfort against my restless thoughts. The season's been a grueling marathon of sweat and sacrifice, each game etching new lines in our story. We're a band of brothers, and now the championship game looms, the proverbial puck at center ice of our fate, ready for the drop. It’s not just any game—it's the culmination of every bruise, every early morning practice, every moment we chose grit over surrender.

"Winning isn't everything," they say, but those folks probably never spent a season with a target on their backs. My teammates, my brothers-in-arms—we've battled through slumps that felt like eternal winters, injuries, and victories that tasted. This last game? It's more than just a game. It’s a chance to prove that our growth wasn’t just luck. And by God, I intend to leave it all on the ice.

Stepping out from the cool confines of the locker room, the energy of the town washes over me. It's palpable, electric, a current that buzzes through the air and invigorates the soul. Fans cluster in huddles of jerseys and painted faces; their cheers and chants rise and fall like waves.

"Go, Sabres!" They roar, voices blending into a harmonious tumult that could stir even the most stoic of hearts. Homemade banners sway in the breeze, splashed with slogans penned in vibrant hues—declarations of loyalty, faith in underdogs turned titans. I smile, a surge of pride swelling within as I acknowledge the love affair between this team and our town.

I adjust my cap, nodding to fans who call out my name. Today, the stakes are higher than ever, but if there's one thing I know about us, it's that we never shy away from the heat of the moment. We skate headfirst into the blaze.

My hands are steady, but my heart? It's racing like it's already mid-game, pounding against my ribs in anticipation. I stand, adjusting the fit of my shoulder pads, ensuring every piece of equipment feels like an extension of myself. Nothing can be out of place—not today.

Glancing up, I catch a ripple of movement by the rink wall near the penalty box. It's Lily, her chestnut hair tied back in a way that makes those green eyes even more piercing. She's laughing with Rodriguez, a hand on his shoulder, no doubt infusing him with her signature blend of optimism and joy. She's always had this uncanny ability to boost morale, as if her belief could seep into your veins and make you better than you thought possible.

Our gazes lock for a moment, and there's a jolt, an electric hum that zips through the air between us. Words hover unsaid, thick with everything that's been brewing off the ice. I'd give anything to cross the distance, to confront the tension head-on, but now's not the time. Not when we have a game to win, not when every second counts.

She nods at me, a silent message of 'go get 'em,' and I nod back, letting out a breath. There's an entire conversation in that exchange, heavy with words we've yet to speak aloud. But right now, I need to channel all this restless energy into the game, into being the defenseman I'm meant to be—focused, unyielding, a pillar for the team.

I take one last deep breath, letting the chill of the rink settle into my lungs, steadying my racing pulse. I'm ready. With each step toward the ice, the sound of the crowd builds, a crescendo of expectation that fills the space around us.

This is it. Game on.

The cold steel of the blade bites into the ice, a crisp sound that's as much a part of me as my own heartbeat. I push off, gliding toward the center circle for the face-off. This game is everything—our season's climax, and now, unknowingly, the prologue to my personal reckoning with Lily.

I nod to myself, more out of habit than anyone else's benefit. I have to be here, fully present on the ice. My team needs Ethan Scott, the defenseman, not a lovelorn fool. So I channel it all—the hope, the fear—into my gameplay.

The puck drops, and instantly, the world narrows to the sounds of the game: the slice of skates, the thwack of sticks, the roar of the crowd. I'm a predator on the hunt, eyes sharp, muscles coiled. Every pass, every check is calculated with strategic precision. I defend our goal like it's my own life on the line, because today, it feels like it is.

"Scott, watch the wing!" Marco's voice cuts through the cacophony, and instinctively, I pivot, blocking an incoming rival with a shoulder that feels like it's made of steel rather than flesh and bone. We move as one organism, my teammates and I, anticipating each other's moves, compensating, covering, attacking.

I leap into action, seizing the puck and sending it hurtling across the ice with a sniper's accuracy toward Lucas, who's breaking away. He catches it, no look, and I know he'll make the shot. As he takes it, I circle back, ready to defend or celebrate—whichever is needed.

My lungs burn with exertion, and the chill of the rink can't cool the fire in my veins. This is where I belong, where every piece of the puzzle that is Ethan Scott fits perfectly. The leader, the protector, the player—all facets of me shine brightest here, on this frozen battlefield.

With each stride, each play, I pour every ounce of my being into the game, because if I can't lay bare my heart to Lily just yet, I'll bare my soul here in the one place I know how—with unwavering determination and an ironclad will to win.

"Scott!" The call for the puck snaps me back, and I'm in motion again, a relentless force driven by more than just the desire to claim victory. This isn't just about hockey anymore—it never really was. Every move, every decision, is playing for more than a win; I'm playing for a chance. And when the time comes to face Lily after the final horn blares, I'll know I left nothing unsaid.

The puck slams against the glass with a bone-rattling thud, and the crowd erupts into a cacophony of cheers and groans. My muscles tense as I track the black disk, every sense sharpened to a razor's edge. The score is tied, and each tick of the clock feels like a heartbeat, loud and insistent in my ears.

"Scott! Defense!" Marco's voice cuts through the noise, pulling me back into formation. I pivot on my skates, watching as their forward barrels toward me, eyes hungry for a goal that I swear he won't get.

I brace myself. This is it—the moment of truth where every second counts, where the thin line between winning and losing is drawn in ice shavings and sweat. Our fans are a blur of colors, but I can hear individual voices—some chanting my name, others screaming strategic obscenities.

I steal a glance at the stands, searching for that familiar face, but there's no time for distraction. Not when every move could tip the scales.

"Stay on him, Scott!" Coach's command snaps my focus back to the game. I zero in on my opponent, reading his body like a book I've studied a thousand times. He fakes left, but I don't bite. I know this dance, the feints and jabs—it's a language spoken in the angle of a wrist and the shift of weight on blades.

He shoots, aiming for the top corner, but I'm there—my stick intercepts the puck. The crowd roars their approval, a wave of sound that crashes over me, fueling the adrenaline that courses through my veins.

"Nice block, Ethan!" Alex yells from the bench, his voice cutting through the din. I can't help the grin that flashes across my face, even as my lungs scream for air and my legs burn with exertion.

This is what it all comes down to—these moments of pure, unadulterated hockey where everything else fades away. Where the pressure is a fire that either forges you into something stronger or reduces you to ashes.

My jersey clings to my back, soaked with perspiration. I can feel the weight of every stride, every check, every pass. My muscles protest, but I push them harder, demanding more because anything less would be a disservice to the team, to the game, to her. And as I steel myself for the next onslaught, I know that no matter how this ends, I'll have played my heart out.

The clock is a merciless god ticking down our fate, seconds slipping away like they're greased. I'm a coiled spring, tension wired through every fiber of my being as the puck slides across the ice with a taunting hiss. Eyes locked on its black silhouette, I anticipate the opposing forward's move—a feint to the left, a deke to the right.

"Scott! Cover the slot!" Coach's voice cuts through the cacophony, sharp and insistent.

I pivot, my skates carving arcs into the ice, positioning myself between the shooter and our net. The stadium vibrates with energy, a living entity echoing the thundering heartbeats of every soul within it. This is it—the apex where glory and defeat balance on the edge of a knife.

"Here it comes!" Marco's warning shout is almost drowned in the uproar, but I catch it, an anchor in the storm.

Time distorts, elongates, turning seconds into minutes into hours. The forward releases a bullet, a blistering shot aimed to exploit the tiny void between our goalie and the post. I lunge, extending every inch of muscle and willpower, my stick an extension of my arm. The puck ricochets off its blade with a gratifying clap, deflecting away from our goal.

"Scott, you beauty!" Alex's cheer pierces the noise.

But there's no time to revel in the save. The puck's still in play, rebounding toward me. Instinct takes over; I corral it with the toe of my blade and look up. There, beyond a maze of sticks and skates, is an opening—a path to victory.

With a burst of speed fueled by sheer grit, I charge forward, breaking through their defensive line like a hurricane through paper. I can hear Lily's voice in my head, spurring me on. The goal looms ahead, a gaping mouth ready to swallow my attempt at glory.

"Go, Ethan, go!" Her voice is clear now, not in my head, but from the stands.

The goalie squares to me, eyes wide, aware that this could be the moment that defines us both. I fake left, pull the puck right, and let it fly. It sails through the air, and—

The buzzer blares. The crowd holds its breath, awaiting the puck's verdict as it hurdles toward the net. Time freezes, the world zeroes in on that piece of vulcanized rubber and the mesh it may or may not kiss.

And then, darkness swallows the arena.

A power outage? In the final seconds?

Disbelief grips me, grips everyone as we stand suspended in uncertainty, the outcome hanging unseen in the shadows.

"Did it go in?" someone yells, the question echoing in the pitch-black.

The last thing I remember before chaos erupts is the weightless sensation of not knowing, of being caught in the limbo between triumph and possible heartache.

CHAPTER TWENTY THREE: MARCO

He made it. Ethan made it.

I shake my head in wonder as we glide back out onto the ice after the power comes back up. We're still down points—and we're down to the wire.

But Ethan was the one who'd put us within reaching distance of a win.

The chill of the rink bites at my skin as I step through the gate, blades biting into the ice with a familiar hiss. The cacophony of the crowd swells around me like a living thing, their combined anticipation sending a shiver down my spine that has nothing to do with the cold. My heart's thumping hard against my chest, a mix of nerves and excitement coursing through my veins. This was it—the culmination of everything we've worked for.

"Go get 'em, Wild Shot!" someone screams from the stands, and I can't suppress the smirk tugging at my lips. They love the nickname almost as much as they love the man behind it—Marco "Wild Shot" Silvestri, the guy who learned to skate before he could run, whose life story is as peppered with drama as the latest tabloid sensation.

The guy who finds himself happy to be here—and not just because of Lily, though there is that. Because I get to be on the ice with the guys surrounding me. I've spent a long time feeling sorry for my past, hurt over my family. But I have a great family, right here.

As the puck drops, something primal takes over. Muscle memory and instinct blend together in a dance I've perfected since those days on inner-city rinks where hockey wasn't just a game. My skates carve the ice, one stroke after another, propelling me forward.

I catch the puck on my stick and it feels like an extension of my arm, alive and eager to play along. With a flick of my wrist, it's off, slicing across the ice toward the net. And then—bam! The sound of success as the puck slams home. A goal. I barely register the roar of the crowd; I'm already circling back, eyes searching for the next opportunity. Tied up isn't a win.

"Silvestri! Here!"

Lucas's voice cuts through the din. I pivot, sending ice crystals flying, and spot him by the boards. A deft pass sends the puck his way, and he's off, dashing toward the opposing team's goal. It's a game of chess played at breakneck speed, and I'm always three moves ahead. Another assist. Then another goal, my stick finding the sweet spot again and again.

Nobody would guess that the guy making these plays is the same one who ducked out of practice early to indulge in temptations that used to lure him into the night. But beneath this olive skin, and behind these brown eyes that have seen more than they should, there's a mind that's sharp as the blades on my skates—a mind that's playing for more than just the win.

As I glide across the ice, every pass, every shot, every strategic move is more than just part of the game. It's a silent shout-out to those kids back home, skating on cracked concrete, dreaming of a future they can hardly imagine. For them, I'll be the exception, the proof that sometimes, even the wildest shots can make it.

The roar of the crowd crescendos into a tangible wave of energy that courses through the arena. "Marco! Marco!" they chant, a rhythmic anthem that fuels my every stride. I can almost feel the vibration of their voices beneath my skates as I weave through defenders, a conductor orchestrating a symphony of anticipation and excitement.

"Wild Shot" — a moniker earned from a past that's still nipping at my heels, a reminder that every slick move is more than just showboating; it's redemption in motion. I sidestep another check, my gaze locked on the net, heart pounding with the drumbeat of the game clock winding down.

"Silvestri scores!" The announcer's voice booms, and the stadium erupts, fans leaping to their feet, banners waving like flags claiming victory. With each goal I've tucked behind the goalie tonight, a weight has lifted.

And then, there it is — the final buzzer, cutting through, a sweet sound signaling triumph. I pump my fist in the air, the satisfaction of the win mingling with the adrenaline still coursing through my veins. My teammates rush toward me, their faces split into wide grins, all sweat and elation as we collide into a jubilant tangle of pads and jerseys. High-fives crackle like static around the huddle, each slap of palm against glove echoing our shared euphoria.

"Great game, Wild Shot!" Ethan slaps my shoulder, his eyes gleaming with the thrill of victory. Lily shoots me a wink from where she leans over the boards, her own smile telling a story of pride and affection. In this moment, surrounded by my team, their joy is my joy, their dreams interwoven with mine in the fabric of this hard-fought win.

***

As the locker room door swings shut behind us, the chorus of cheers from the ice fades into a distant hum. My heart is a drumbeat, thumping against my ribs with a rhythm that matches my steps. The post-match interviews loom ahead like an open net, an opportunity to score something much more significant than a game-winning goal.

"Hey, Marco, you ready to light up the mic like you did the ice?" Ethan tosses me a towel, his grin as infectious as it was during our on-ice celebration.

"Always," I shoot back, though my voice doesn't carry the usual confidence. It's not the glare of the spotlight that has my nerves dancing — it's the weight of what I'm about to reveal. I pull off my helmet, feeling the sticky cling of sweat in my hair.

I slip out of the bustle of the locker room, each step toward the interview room peeling away another layer of the hockey star persona. Marco "Wild Shot" Silvestri, they call me, but tonight, it's Marco the man who needs to take the stage.

The door to the interview room opens, and I'm greeted by the stark brightness of camera lights and the low murmur of reporters shuffling papers, adjusting lenses. My palms are slightly sweaty; I wipe them on the sides of my suit pants, a nervous gesture hidden from the prying eyes that wait beyond the threshold. I've faced down goalies with less trepidation than this.

"Mr. Silvestri, right this way," a producer beckons, and I follow her cue, settling into the chair that feels more like a hot seat. Microphones stand at attention before me, a silent audience awaiting my words. Deep breath in, deep breath out.

The microphone feels something I know how to handle, yet it's never been quite this heavy. The interviewer, a guy with a sharp suit and sharper gaze, leans in, his question slicing through the buzz of anticipation that's more deafening than the cheers from the ice.

"Marco, you were on fire out there tonight! What's going through your mind when you're racking up those points?"

I flash a grin, the kind that's won me as many fans as my stickhandling. "Ah, it's not just me out there, you know? Hockey's a team sport." I lean back, feeling the warmth of the spotlight. "It's the passes from my linemates, the defense keeping our net clear, and the coach's strategies. I'm just the guy lucky enough to end up with the puck at the right moment."

The interviewer nods, scribbling something down, but I'm not done yet. There's a mission pulsing in my veins, stronger than the adrenaline from the game. With a smile playing on my lips, I decide it's time to drop the gloves on something that's been shadowing me, much like I shadow the goal before a shot.

"You know," I begin, the cameras zooming in, "scoring goals isn't the only way I'm hoping to make an impact." A beat of silence, and I can almost hear the collective lean-in of the audience. "Back in my old neighborhood, we didn't have much, but we had a community rink—a place where dreams weren't just about playing, but making it somewhere else—making it out."

The interviewer's eyes widen slightly, the pen pausing mid-air.

"I've been quietly funding scholarships for the kids in my old neighborhood. They deserve a shot, you know? Not just at hockey, but at whatever dreams they've got." My voice is steady, but the Italian lilt of my heritage colors the words with the hues of home—the same streets that toughened me up and taught me about real goals, the kind that don't light up a scoreboard.

There's no playbook for this moment, no drills that could've prepared me for the vulnerability of laying bare part of my soul before millions. But then again, I've always played best off-script.

"Growing up," I say, my voice cutting through the stillness, "the rink was my sanctuary. It was more than just a slab of frozen water; it was where I learned about life's offsides and power plays. It was where I escaped a home full of violence and anger." There's a warmth in my chest that grows with every word, a fire that's been stoked by memories of cold mornings and the sound of pucks against chain-link fences.

"Those kids, they're fighting more battles than what you see on the ice—they're dodging more than just the other players." My hands gesture on their own accord, as if they're illustrating the story of every kid who laced up a pair of skates with dreams bigger than their worn-out gear.

"Every goal I score, every game we win, it's not just for the team—it's for them. Because someone has to show these kids that the game isn't over after the third period. That there's overtime in life, and sometimes, that's where the real victories happen." The pride swelling within me is from the thought of those scholarships turning dead-end streets into avenues of possibility.

"Sure, I'm known for my wild shots," I continue with a half-cocked grin, letting a slice of my mischievous side show. "For my bad behavior sometimes. But maybe it's time I'm known for something else, too—like giving these kids a shot at a future they never dared to dream of."

I lean back in my chair, the leather sticking slightly to my damp jersey. The questions will come fast and curious, but for now, I've said my piece. And it feels like lighting the lamp in a sudden-death shootout—exhilarating, revealing, victorious.

The adrenaline is still humming in my veins when I spot her in the back of the room, leaning against the wall with that familiar half-smile. Lily's here. She's trying to be discreet, but she might as well be a spotlight in a dark rink—she draws the eye.

"Before we wrap this up," I say, feeling a grin tug at the corner of my mouth, "I've got one more thing." My heart's pounding.

"Um, yeah?" The interviewer looks up, clearly not expecting another headline from me tonight.

I take a deep breath, and the words come out steady, fueled by something much deeper than confidence. "This incredible woman back here," I tilt my head toward Lily, feeling every muscle in my body tense with anticipation, "this is Lily Morgan, and she's my girlfriend."

It's like scoring a buzzer-beater, that moment. Our eyes lock across the crowded room, hers wide with surprise and excitement, mine probably shining with all the affection I feel for her. There's no hiding behind helmets and plexiglass now; this is us, Marco and Lily, no aliases or pretenses.

A collective inhale sucks the air from the room, and then it's chaos—applause, gasps, whispers ricocheting off the walls like a rogue puck. Cameras lift, shutters click rapidly, and I can almost hear the tweets being crafted in real-time. "Hockey's Wild Shot Scores Off the Ice" headlines are already writing themselves.

Lily's cheeks turn the red of our team jerseys, but she holds my gaze, a silent communication passing between us. And just like that, our private world becomes infinitely larger, shared with fans and strangers alike.

"Marco Silvestri, not just making plays on the ice, but also in love," someone quips from the back, eliciting laughter that ripples through the room.

"Hey," I shoot back, my voice laced with mock indignation, "I'll have you know, Lily's the one who made the first move."

"Did not!" Lily's sharp retort floats above the noise, and the room erupts again, this time with the warmth of shared amusement.

"Agree to disagree," I reply, my smile unwavering. It's a scene straight out of the rom-com playbook, but it's ours, unscripted and undeniably real. I hold out my hand, and she comes my way to take it.

The air is charged, a current of energy that buzzes through my veins as I tighten my grip on Lily's hand. Her fingers lace with mine, a tangible reminder that we're taking this leap together. It's out there now, our relationship; no more hiding in the shadows of secret rendezvous and whispered promises. This is it—the big reveal—and my heart feels like it's going to burst right out of my chest with pride.

"Marco," Lily whispers, "you did it."

I glance at her, her gaze mirroring the exhilaration I feel. "We did it," I correct her, because this isn't just my victory or my moment. It's ours. And damn, does it feel good to finally be able to say it—to scream it from the rooftops if I want.

As the interview wraps up, I stand, pulling Lily up with me. We're a team, and as we leave the interview room, the excited crowd parts for us like the Red Sea. Their cheers fill the air, a chorus of enthusiasm that follows us out. We move past them, our steps light—almost buoyant—as if we're skating on air rather than walking on carpet.

"Think they took it well?" Lily jests, a radiant smile spreading across her face, showcasing a dimple that I find absolutely captivating every single time it makes an appearance.

"Better than well," I reply, grinning back at her. "They're eating it up. You're probably trending online already, love."

"Again?" she quips, her tone laced with sarcasm, but there's a sparkle in her eye that gives away her true feelings.

"Come on, let's get out of here before they start asking for autographs," I suggest, nodding toward the locker room. But really, what I'm thinking is how much I want to be alone with her, to savor this moment just a little bit longer without the world watching.

"Your wish is my command," she says, playing along with the light-hearted banter we've perfected over time.

"Is it now?" I tease, leaning in close enough that only she can hear. "Remind me to make a few more wishes later."

Lily laughs, the sound musical and light, and honestly, I could listen to it forever. The thought hits me suddenly, unbidden, but not unwelcome. Forever with Lily Morgan—it has a nice ring to it. But that's a thought for another day. For now, there's just this—her hand in mine, the buzz of a crowd still chanting my name, and the warmth of knowing that when the lights go down and the ice melts away, I'll have her by my side.

And that's the kind of win you can't put on a scoreboard.

CHAPTER TWENTY FOUR: LILY

My pulse is a drumline, out of sync and way too loud, as I push through the door into the cool confines of the locker room. Marco follows, and it's like stepping onto the ice before a big game, except there are no cheering fans or eager teammates—just Ethan, standing there like a pillar of my personal pantheon of complicated feelings.

"Hey," I manage, my voice sounding unnaturally high in my own ears.

Marco leans back against a row of lockers, his arms folded across his chest. His dark hair is a tousled mess, opposite of the rigid set of his jaw. He gives me a nod that's both encouragement and challenge rolled into one.

Ethan's blue eyes catch mine for a moment, searching as if he's trying to read the play before it unfolds. There's something about the way he stands, both relaxed and ready, that makes me think of those moments on the ice when the puck is up for grabs and everything hangs in balance.

"Hey, Lily, Marco," Ethan says, his voice steady and calm, but I can hear the question behind it. He's always been able to do that—say one thing and mean another without ever being disingenuous. It's part of what makes him such a formidable defenseman; he's a master at anticipation.

They exchange a look over my head, quick and unreadable. I'm not sure what silent conversation passes between them, but it's enough to crank the tension up a notch. I stand there, caught in the middle, with my heart hammering away and knowing that whatever happens next could change the game for all of us.

I square my shoulders, feeling Marco's intense gaze at my back and Ethan's cool scrutiny from the front. The locker room suddenly feels smaller, the scent of exertion and ice wax potent in the air. I can practically hear each tick of the clock on the wall, counting down to a moment I've both dreaded and longed for.

"Okay," I begin, my voice steady despite the tempest inside me. "Ethan, there's something you need to know about Marco and me." I pause, searching for the right words, wanting to be as transparent as the ice we battle on but without causing fractures in our team's unity. "We're... together."

The words hang between us, suspended like a puck mid-air before a critical shot. I rush to fill the silence, to explain before misunderstandings take root. "We chose not to tell anyone because we didn't want it to become a distraction."

Next to me, Marco shifts his weight, his presence a solid reassurance. "Yeah, we thought it was best to keep it on the down-low," he says, his Italian accent coloring the words with a warmth that does little to ease the tension.

I glance at him, grateful for his support not just in our relationship but also in the philosophy we share: the team comes first. It's one of the things that drew me to him, this hotshot forward who plays with such passion and yet understands the delicate balance of personal desires and professional commitments.

"We wanted to wait until after the season," I add. "To avoid any potential... complications."

My voice trails off, but the unspoken words linger, heavy with implication.

Ethan's eyes, those bright blue windows to his soul, don't waver from mine, but something shifts behind them. A shadow of something lost, a glimmer of something forlorn—it flickers by so fast I wonder if I've imagined it. But I know Ethan, the way he can hide a world of emotion behind that stalwart gaze, and I'm certain I've caught a glimpse of disappointment.

"Understandable," he says, his voice measured, betraying none of the storm I just saw brewing in his eyes

He steps forward, offering a nod that might as well be a pat on the back after a solid play. There's a smile there too, small and maybe not entirely reaching his eyes, but it's genuine enough to tug at my conscience. He extends this olive branch to Marco first, then me. "You guys make a good team," he adds, and I hear the double meaning loud and clear. We're more than just a couple—we're part of his team, and that's sacred ground to Ethan Scott.

My chest tightens with relief and regret. Relief because Ethan isn't letting personal feelings ice over what we've built. Regret because, beneath his supportive exterior, I know we've just added another layer of complexity to the intricate dance of our friendship.

"Thanks, Ethan," Marco chimes in, his tone lighter, almost grateful. "We're all in this together, right? For the win?"

"Always for the win," Ethan affirms, his eyes finally breaking away from mine to glance at the row of lockers behind us, each one holding a story, a struggle, a dream. His jaw sets firmly, and I recognize that determined tilt of his head. It's the same look he gets right before a critical defensive play, when he's about to shut down the opposing team's best scorer.

The chill of the locker room wraps around me like a shroud. Ethan stands there, an immovable force, his broad shoulders squared as if he's ready to defend against life's slap shots just as skillfully as he does on the ice.

"Look, Lily," he starts, and I brace myself for the slap of his words. But they come out soft, almost gentle, which somehow makes this whole thing even more difficult. "I want you to know—I turned down the transfer. Not because I didn't want the opportunity, but because this is where I want to be."

I blink, trying to process the weight of that decision. It's not just about the team; it's about loyalty, sacrifice. It's about Ethan.

"Staying here means something to me," he continues, his bright blue eyes locking onto mine with an intensity that pins me in place. "We've built something important. And I'm not just talking about what happens on the ice. Our dreams, the community we've rallied... it's bigger than any one game, any one season."

There's a lump forming in my throat, a tight ball of emotion that makes it hard to swallow. His conviction hammers at me, each word another reminder of his steadfastness. The shadows under his eyes speak of sleepless nights spent weighing his options, but he doesn't regret his choice. He's chosen us, chosen the team over a possibly shinier future elsewhere.

Admiration swells within me, a tide of respect for the man before me who embodies everything a team could want in a player—a leader. And yet, nestled among those cresting waves of respect, is sadness, deep and aching. Sadness because I know what it's like to put everything aside for the sake of the team, to bury personal desires beneath the weight of collective goals.

"Thanks, Ethan," Marco says. "That means a lot. To all of us."

He nods, a simple gesture, but it's filled with the quiet strength that defines him. Ethan Scott is the kind of guy who puts others first, who stands strong when the pressure mounts. And in that moment, as I stand there grappling with my own tangled feelings, I realize just how lucky we are to have him on our side.

"Thank you," I murmur, my voice thick with gratitude and something else—something that feels dangerously close to vulnerability. "Really, Ethan, for understanding... for being here."

His muscles tense beneath my touch, not flinching, but bracing. And then he relaxes, turns to me, blue eyes locking onto mine with an intensity that does funny things to my heart rate. Ethan is someone who I know is going to meet his match someday—and, boy, is that woman going to not know what hit her.

"Hey," he says softly, giving me a smile that somehow manages to be both reassuring and heartbreakingly genuine. "I've got your back, Lily. Yours and the team's. No matter what the scoreboard says."

In that moment, with his smile cutting through the tension like a skate blade across fresh ice, I believe him. I believe in the strength of his support, in the steadfast nature of his loyalty. A silence descends upon us—a thick, palpable hush that seems to make the locker room shrink. I can feel Marco's gaze on me, heavy with unspoken thoughts, while Ethan's blue eyes remain steady, holding a trace of something undefinable.

Whatever happens, I know one thing for sure: the game goes on, and so must I. No matter how our relationships evolve, I'm determined to ensure we can all hold our heads high, proud of the way we played the game. Together.

CHAPTER TWENTY FIVE: LILY

The air crackles with the kind of anticipation that usually precedes a big game as I push open the heavy door to the local community center. It's not the scent of fresh ice or the chill of a rink that greets me, though; it's the antiseptic tang of polished linoleum and the distant echo of children's laughter from some far-off room. But the feeling is familiar all the same—excitement laced with nerves.

I'm here to help orchestrate a charity event, and Marco, with his mess of dark hair and easy charm, is my unexpected partner in this endeavor. My fingers fidget at my sides, betraying my cool demeanor.

"Looking for someone?"

I spin around, nearly losing my balance, but strong hands steady me. I look up into a pair of deep brown eyes that seem to twinkle with mischief. It's Marco, of course. Those hands are a dead giveaway — scarred and rough from years of gripping hockey sticks.

"So," Marco says, clapping his hands together, "we have a lot to cover. Sponsors, volunteers, auction items..."

"Marketing strategies, outreach programs..." I chime in, my mind already racing with possibilities. Ideas flow between us like a well-executed play, each suggestion met with thoughtful consideration or playful counter.

"Who knew we'd make such a good team off the ice?" Marco grins, nudging me with his elbow.

"Let's not get ahead of ourselves," I reply, though I can't deny the synergy sparking between us. "We haven't even started yet."

"True," Marco concedes, "but something tells me we're going to knock this out of the park. Or should I say, out of the rink?"

"Stick to hockey metaphors, Wild Shot," I laugh, shaking my head. "They suit you better."

"Fair enough, Morgan," he says with a wink. "Let's get to work then, shall we?"

"Let's."

The sound of laughter echoes through the community center's hall as we set up booths for the charity gala. My hands are busy tying red and gold ribbons – our team colors – around the backs of chairs, but my mind is on the people these preparations are for. A little boy with a mop of curly hair grins up at me as I hand him a balloon, his eyes sparkling with the kind of joy that only comes from simple pleasures.

"Thank you!" he chirps, clutching the string tightly.

"Anytime, champ," I reply, ruffling his hair. "Are you going to show us your hockey skills later?"

He nods vigorously. "I'm gonna score a hundred goals!" His determination reminds me of someone else I know.

"Make it a hundred and one," Marco chimes in, appearing beside us with a stack of bakery boxes. The boy giggles and races off. I watch him go, feeling a surge of warmth. This is why we're doing this – for moments like that.

"Marco, you've got a way with kids," I say, impressed despite myself.

"Ah, they're just mini versions of us, right?" He winks, then hands me a pastry out of the top box. "Speaking of which, we should start setting up the auction items. I'm going to make sure everyone gets a snack."

"Good idea." I move toward the entrance, pausing only to throw back at Marco, "You're becoming quite the out-front philanthropist, Mr. Silvestri."

Marco's brown eyes gleam with a light that speaks volumes of his newfound purpose.

"Can't let you have all the fun," he retorts, his eyes meeting mine with that mischievous glint I've come to adore. "

I love this side of him—the planner, the dreamer, the man who's as passionate about making a difference as he is about hockey. It's a side few get to see, masked beneath his playful bravado. He's all smiles and charm, but there's no missing the sincerity in his actions.

Marco's gaze fixes abruptly on me. He hesitates for a moment, handing off the bakery boxes to a nearby woman. Then, suddenly, he rushes back over to me.

I forgot something," he confesses, concern etched on his handsome features.

"Forgot what?" I ask, puzzled. "I think we've got everything covered."

His eyes meet mine and he takes a deep breath. "No, we missed one thing... one thing that would make this gala the best." He takes my hands in his, much to my surprise. "The most important piece."

"And that would be?" I prompt him when he doesn't immediately elaborate.

"A dance," he says, a playful smirk on his lips. "Every gala needs a dance. And I know just the song."

I blink in surprise, my heart pounding as he raises one of my hands and places the other around his neck. "Marco, we are in the middle of setting up—"

"But everyone's on break now," Marco remarks, glancing around at the volunteers scattered across the room, chatting and munching on pastries. He turns back to me, a devilish glint in his eyes. "So…"

Before I can protest any further, he starts moving, leading us into an impromptu dance, right here in the middle of the community center. His movements are fluid and confident, reflecting his adeptness on the ice.

"Marco!" I protest weakly, yet I laugh, caught up in the spontaneity of his gesture.

"Shush, Lily," he admonishes gently. "Just follow my lead." So I do, and it doesn't take long for me to fall into rhythm with him. Our bodies sway in time with an imagined melody, my heart beating a tattoo against my ribs.

As we dance, I notice how different Marco is off the ice – a little softer around the edges, a little more carefree. His dark eyes sparkle with unguarded affection, a smile tugging at his lips as he twirls me around. "You're quite the dancer, Miss Morgan," he mumbles, his voice husky, and I feel my cheeks flush at his compliment.

"I'm all right," I laugh, trying to downplay the heat I feel rising in my cheeks. Marco merely chuckles, drawing me closer so our bodies are nearly touching. It sends a jolt of electricity through my body and for a moment I am lost in the intensity of his gaze.

"So humble," he teases, his lips quirking up in a smile. "You're more than all right, Lily. And not just at dancing."

His words leave an echo in my ear, an echo that spreads through my body like a chord resonating on a guitar. He's close, so close that I can smell the faint scent of his cologne - crisp and masculine - mixed with the earthy scent of baked goods from his earlier bakery run.

It's intoxicating. But it's not just the scent that's making my head spin - it's the heat of his body, the intensity of his gaze. It's him. It's Marco Silvestri, the hotshot forward with the devilish grin and eyes that hold a world of secrets.

Our dance ends too quickly, but Marco doesn't let go. Instead, he keeps me close, his hands gently resting on my waist. His eyes search mine, and the atmosphere between us changes. The playful banter is replaced by a powerful silence.

"I..." he starts but seems to struggle to find his words. I stay silent, waiting for him to continue, my heartbeat a steady rhythm in my ears. After a moment, he swallows hard and his gaze intensifies.

"I need to tell you something, Lily," he says softly, his voice barely above a whisper. I can see the vulnerability in his eyes, the apprehension. It's not like him to be this serious; it sends a flutter of anticipation through me.

"What is it, Marco?" I ask, trying to keep my voice steady. His fingers tighten around mine, sending a flurry of sparks up my arm.

He takes a deep breath, holding my gaze with an intensity that makes my heart skip a beat. "I love you Lily," he says, the words falling from his lips like a secret that's been held captive for far too long. The intensity in his eyes is replaced by an indescribable tenderness, an emotion so raw and poignant that it leaves me speechless.

"You...what?" I stammer, my mind reeling. Marco doesn't falter, though. His gaze remains fixed, burning with sincerity.

"I love you, Lily," he repeats, his voice stronger now. He reaches up to gently tuck a loose strand of hair behind my ear. His touch sends tingles down my spine as I try to process the words that just left his lips.

"I've been trying to get up the nerve to tell you for a while," he continues, "but I never seemed to find the right moment. Until now." His thumb gently strokes my cheek, making me shiver with a mixture of surprise and pleasure. "I know this is sudden, but...you mean everything to me, Lily."

His words hang in the air between us, his confession sending my thoughts into a whirlwind. The room around us fades into an unimportant blur as the magnitude of his declaration sinks in. I've watched him grow from a wild child into the dedicated hockey player he is today, and it has been a journey.

A journey filled with laughter, challenges, and unexpected moments of vulnerability, like the one we're sharing now. My heart, once racing with anticipation, now swells with an emotion so profound, so encompassing, it's almost overwhelming. Marco Silvestri, the man who's always been larger than life, stands before me, raw and open, his heart laid bare.

For a long moment, I'm lost for words, caught in the tide of my own emotions that mirror his. The realization hits me with the force of a slap shot—my feelings for Marco have deepened beyond the playful banter and the competitive spark that initially drew us together. They've grown into something more, something real and all-consuming.

The silence stretches between us, but it's not uncomfortable. It's charged with the weight of his words, the sincerity in his gaze. And then, as if propelled by a force greater than myself, I find my voice.

"I love you too, Marco," I whisper, the words tumbling out in a breathless rush. It feels like a release, like I'm finally allowing myself to acknowledge the depth of my feelings for him.

Marco's reaction is immediate; his eyes light up, a mix of relief and joy transforming his face. And then, he's leaning in, his lips finding mine in a kiss that seals our confessions. It's gentle at first, a tentative exploration that soon grows more passionate, more assured. This kiss is different from any other—it's a promise, a vow made without words, a bridge between two hearts that have finally found their way to each other.

As we break apart, breathless and with hearts pounding, I smile. The world outside the arena, with all its rivalries and games, fades into insignificance. In this moment, it's just Marco and me, united by a love that feels as inevitable as it is surprising.

And as we stand, hand in hand, ready to face whatever comes next, I know that together, we're unstoppable.

NOW AVAILABLE!

PUCKER UP
(A Silverpeak Sabres College Hockey Romance—Book 2)

When the Silverpeak Sabres find themselves facing a publicity for their bad-boy image, they need to bring in outside help: undergrad journalist Fiona Harper. But Fiona finds herself in hot water when she writes a scathing article about the team and, forced to follow and report on the season, she soon finds herself in an enemies-to-lovers situation with not one but two star players: responsible defenseman Noah, and smug forward Lucas.

PUCKER UP: SILVERPEAK SABRES HOCKEY BOOK 2 is the second book in an enthralling new sports romance series filled with witty humor, heartfelt moments, sensual subplots, and unexpected twists. Prepare to be captivated by alluring new protagonists in each book that are ready to capture your interest and keep you turning pages well into the night.

Future books in the series are also available!

Audrey Shine

Audrey Shine is author of the JULIET PAGE COZY MYSTERY series, comprising five books (and counting); and of the new SILVERPEAK SABRES ROMANCE series, comprising five books (and counting).

Audrey would love to hear from you, so please visit www.audreyshineauthor.com to receive free ebooks, hear the latest news, and stay in touch.

BOOKS BY AUDREY SHINE

JULIET PAGE COZY MYSTERY
A HARDCOVER HOMICIDE (Book #1)
A LETHAL LEXICON (Book #2)
A VOLUME IN VENGEANCE (Book #3)
A TYPESET TRAGEDY (Book #4)
A FATAL FOOTNOTE (Book #5)

SILVERPEAK SABRES ROMANCE
GOOD PUCK CHARM (Book #1)
PUCKER UP (Book #2)
NAUGHTY & ICE (Book #3)
PUCK OF THE DRAW (Book #4)
HEARTS ON ICE (Book #5)

Printed in Great Britain
by Amazon

43717638R00088